"I have to protect my son."

His black eyes burned like coal. "You think I'm going to hurt Gabe?"

Emma steeled herself. She'd hoped she could get rid of Rafe so she could think, so she wouldn't have to tell him—yet—about Gabe. She'd wanted to protect her son at least another day.

But now she had to tell him. She had to get it over with. Get everything out in the open.

"You've already hurt him, by leaving him when he was inside me. By going off on a dangerous assignment, even when I begged you not to go. Your work was more important to you than me." She blinked back the tears stinging her eyes. "More important than your child."

Rafe's dark face went white. "My...child?"

"He's yours, Rafe. Gabe is your son."

Dear Reader,

In May 2000 Silhouette Romance will commemorate its twentieth anniversary! This line has always celebrated the essence of true love in a manner that blends classic themes and the challenges of romance in today's world into a reassuring, fulfilling novel. From the enchantment of first love to the wonder of second chance, a Silhouette Romance novel demonstrates the power of genuine emotion and the breathless connection that develops between a man and a woman as they discover each other. And this month's stellar selections are quintessential Silhouette Romance stories!

If you've been following LOVING THE BOSS, you'll be amazed when mysterious Rex Barrington III is unmasked in *I Married the Boss!* by Laura Anthony. In this month's FABULOUS FATHERS offering by Donna Clayton, a woman discovers *His Ten-Year-Old Secret*. And opposites attract in *The Rancher and the Heiress,* the third of Susan Meier's TEXAS FAMILY TIES miniseries.

WRANGLERS & LACE returns with Julianna Morris's *The Marriage Stampede.* In this appealing story, a cowgirl butts heads—and hearts—with a bachelor bent on staying that way. Sally Carleen unveils the first book in her exciting duo ON THE WAY TO A WEDDING... with the tale of a twin mistaken for an M.D.'s *Bride in Waiting!* It's both a blessing and a dilemma for a single mother when she's confronted with an amnesiac *Husband Found,* this month's FAMILY MATTERS title by Martha Shields.

Enjoy the timeless power of Romance this month, and every month—you won't be disappointed!

Mary-Theresa Hussey
Mary-Theresa Hussey
Senior Editor, Silhouette Romance

Please address questions and book requests to:
Silhouette Reader Service
U.S.: 3010 Walden Ave., P.O. Box 1325, Buffalo, NY 14269
Canadian: P.O. Box 609, Fort Erie, Ont. L2A 5X3

HUSBAND FOUND

Martha Shields

Silhouette

ROMANCE™

Published by Silhouette Books

America's Publisher of Contemporary Romance

To my sister, Nona.
Though we fought like cats and dogs,
you never got tired of my stories.

 SILHOUETTE BOOKS

ISBN 0-373-19377-7

HUSBAND FOUND

Copyright © 1999 by Martha Shields

All rights reserved. Except for use in any review, the reproduction or utilization of this work in whole or in part in any form by any electronic, mechanical or other means, now known or hereafter invented, including xerography, photocopying and recording, or in any information storage or retrieval system, is forbidden without the written permission of the editorial office, Silhouette Books, 300 East 42nd Street, New York, NY 10017 U.S.A.

All characters in this book have no existence outside the imagination of the author and have no relation whatsoever to anyone bearing the same name or names. They are not even distantly inspired by any individual known or unknown to the author, and all incidents are pure invention.

This edition published by arrangement with Harlequin Books S.A.

® and TM are trademarks of Harlequin Books S.A., used under license. Trademarks indicated with ® are registered in the United States Patent and Trademark Office, the Canadian Trade Marks Office and in other countries.

Look us up on-line at: http://www.romance.net

Printed in U.S.A.

MARTHA SHIELDS

grew up telling stories to her sister to pass the time on the long drives to their grandparents' house. Since she's never been able to stop dreaming up characters, she's thrilled to share her stories with a wider audience. Martha lives in Memphis, Tennessee, with her husband, teenage daughter and a cairn "terror" who keeps trying to live up to his Toto ancestry. Martha has a master's degree in journalism and works at a local university, where her job includes graphic design.

Dear Reader,

I'm happy to bring you one of the books in this special FAMILY MATTERS series. Families, after all, are the bedrock of our society. The firm foundation of family ties gives us the confidence and strength to build happy, healthy lives.

Even when time brings changes—when parents or grandparents or spouses are gone—their love, their teaching, their strength live on. Years later we can still hear them talking to us. We still rely on the advice they gave. We can still feel their love.

In *Husband Found,* Emma Lockwood thinks she has lost the husband she still loves. In the intervening years, she has worked hard to build a solid family life for her fatherless son. Then the husband she thought dead reappears, shaking the foundation of her life and forcing her to redefine her family once again.

I hope you enjoy Emma and Rafe's story. I also hope you enjoy your own family as much as I do mine. I could not wish you any greater happiness.

Love,

Martha

Chapter One

Emma Lockwood caught sight of herself in a mirror as she entered the lobby of the extended-stay motel in east Memphis.

She looked as nervous as she felt. The high spots of color on her cheeks could be explained by too much blush, but the chewed-off lipstick was a dead giveaway. Better freshen up. She didn't need to look desperate for this job.

She balanced her portfolio on a narrow table, then dug her lipstick out of her purse.

Night-time graphics jobs didn't grow on trees in Memphis, so when she'd seen the ad in the *Commercial Appeal,* she'd mailed in her résumé and had been called for an interview. She just hoped this guy's idea of "flexible hours" were the same as hers.

After reapplying her lipstick and dropping it back in her purse, Emma straightened the jacket of her dark red suit. What she looked like shouldn't matter. It was the samples of work in her portfolio that counted. Still, it couldn't hurt to look her best.

She had confidence she could get this job if she wanted it. And she did—as long as the job was legitimate and this guy wasn't some weirdo.

David Johnson. She glanced at the name her mother had written on the notepaper.

Memories flooded through her like they always did when the name Johnson popped up. Bittersweet memories. Memories of three short months in her life when she'd been wonderfully, gloriously, completely happy.

Without thinking, Emma's hand touched the ring hidden beneath her blouse. A class ring from the University of Texas, which had served as her wedding ring for the month she'd been Mrs. Rafe Johnson. She could still—

With an impatient huff, Emma pulled her hand away from her chest and shoved the memories aside. She couldn't get emotional every time she heard the name Johnson. If the pages and pages of them in the Memphis phone book were any indication, it was one of the most common names in America.

She needed to focus on this interview so she could earn enough money for a new roof.

Resolutely she picked up her portfolio and asked the desk clerk for directions to the conference room where the interview would be conducted.

A minute later, she knocked on the door. "Mr. Johnson?"

"Come in," a gravelly voice bade.

Emma straightened her jacket one last time and opened the door to see a man rising from a chair at the other end of a small conference table. She walked forward, extending her hand. "Mr. Johnson, I'm Emma Lockwood. I hope I'm not too early. Your message said—"

Both Emma and her words stopped abruptly as the dark-haired man straightened and extended his hand.

She gasped.

It couldn't be.

They'd only been together three months, and married only a few hours before he left, but she knew his face as well as she knew her son's. Because it was the same one—from the black hair to the black eyes; from the thin, slightly prominent nose to the cleft in the chin. The only differences were the jagged scar running from the corner of this man's left eye down to his blunt jaw and the fine web of wrinkles around his mouth, as if he'd endured too much pain.

It was as if thinking about him had conjured his ghost. She couldn't seem to catch a breath, and her vision narrowed to a tunnel connecting their eyes. "Rafe?"

His eyes widened with a stricken expression. "Do I know you?"

His voice was different—deeper, with the quality of a brook running over stones—but her soul knew the sound.

That same brook roared in her ears. Her purse and portfolio fell from her numb hands, and she took two staggering steps toward him before her world turned black.

Rafe caught the woman before she sank to the floor, though in the process he rammed his hip into the corner of the table, sending pain knifing down his bum leg. He hooked an arm under her knees and lifted her, ignoring the pain as he always did.

Stunned, all he could do was stare.

She'd used his first name, a name he hadn't gone by in years.

Was it possible he knew her? Her pale face, with its small, pert nose, wide mouth and slanted eyes weren't familiar. But then, who had he recognized in the six years since he'd been back? Not even his own parents.

Without warning, a picture popped into his head.

He stood on the bank of the Mississippi River, his arms around a younger version of this same woman.

Smiling shyly, she handed him a folded piece of notebook paper.

"Is this my Thanksgiving present?" he teased, releasing his hold on her to open the paper.

She wrinkled her nose. "You're leaving me for four whole days to eat turkey with your parents all the way down in Houston.

Why would I reward you?'' She gave a tiny shrug. ''This is just a doodle, courtesy of the snoozefest in Dr. Hoffman's class.''

He opened it and burst into laughter. She'd drawn him as his archangel namesake, complete with white robe and wings. A prominent heart on his chest bore the letters EKG.

Rafe drew a finger down her nose. ''How many times have I told you I'm no angel?''

''I know you're not perfect, but you're my guardian angel,'' she said breathlessly. ''So I drew you with broken wings.''

The vision cleared. Paralyzed by shock, Rafe couldn't breathe, though his heart was pounding like a heavy metal drummer on speed.

A memory. It had to be.

A door in his mind had opened for a few, brief seconds, then slammed shut so soundly he couldn't even tell where the door was, much less open it again.

Then the significance of the memory hit him. This woman must be the one who had drawn the picture they'd found clenched in his hand when his almost-dead body had been pulled out of a tree by men in a remote Nicaraguan village. The picture he'd carried for six years. The one that even now had a permanent place in his wallet. The only tangible link to his past.

Staggered by the implications, he focused his eyes on the woman he held. Her honey-gold hair spilled over his arm. Her delicate features were ashen. Who was she? What had she been to him? Girlfriend? Lover? The easy way he remembered touching her suggested intimacy.

He remembered. That in itself was a miracle.

Noticing her head was thrown back at an odd angle, he walked to the couch—his gait more uneven than usual—and laid her down as carefully as if she were a ticking bomb.

But that's exactly what she was. Just touching her had already felt like an explosion. What would happen when she talked to him?

Rafe stood abruptly and limped to the other end of the room, his mind in turmoil.

He'd wakened in a hellhole of a Nicaraguan village six years ago and spent nineteen months in constant pain from the wounds that wouldn't heal, in constant torment from not knowing who he was or where he came from. It was as if his mind had been wiped clean. Oh, he knew how to talk and how to feed and dress himself. He could write, read and speak two languages. But all of his personal information was gone, as if he were a baby starting fresh.

He hadn't even recognized his father when Edward Johnson finally found him and carried him home to Houston. He didn't recognize his mother, his two brothers or his sister, his grandparents, his friends. They'd all taken turns telling him about his life—what he'd liked to eat, pranks he'd pulled, his childhood accomplishments, articles he'd written. They'd even shown him pictures.

But the "memories" they'd instilled in his head didn't feel like this. They weren't three dimensional. They didn't include sounds and smells.

Rafe turned and drove both hands back through his hair as he gazed at the lovely, utterly still woman on the couch.

Those memories hadn't included her.

Why? And what would happen if he touched her again?

Slowly, as if drawn by a fire whose warmth he hadn't felt in eons, he approached her. He pulled over a chair from the conference table and sat. And stared.

He'd waited, hoped, prayed, begged God for this day. Now he wasn't sure he was ready for it. Half of him wanted to shake her awake and demand to know what she knew. The other half wanted to run screaming from the room.

Which was stupid. He'd hoped this would happen. It's why he'd returned to Memphis. This was where he'd lived before he took the assignment to Nicaragua. Since he couldn't find his past in Houston where he grew up, he hoped Memphis was where the answers would be.

But would he like the answers to all of his questions?

He might, if this woman had anything to do with them.

Leaning his elbows on his knees, he slowly extended a finger toward her smooth, pale cheek. He wanted to touch her again, but not to see if she would conjure more memories. He wanted to see if her skin was as soft as it looked—like the petals of the gardenia flowers in his mother's garden.

As he reached for her, he caught sight of his trembling hand. The ugly red scars across the back stopped him cold. He was an aberration, a freak, scarred on the inside and out. Half a man with half a mind.

No wonder she'd fainted. Like Beauty when she saw the Beast.

The thought of being the monster in the fairy tale cut him like a freshly sharpened knife. To stave off the painful notion, he concentrated on the beauty stretched out before him.

What was her name again?

Emma. Emma Lockwood.

He let the syllables echo around his brain. He thought they struck a familiar chord, but he couldn't be sure it wasn't wishful thinking.

Before he could talk himself out of it again, he drew a finger down the cool velvet of her cheek.

Her eyes were like a cat's, slanted and green with tiny flecks of gold. They regarded him with an awe that robbed him of breath.

"Emma," he whispered.

"Kiss me," she demanded, standing on tiptoe.

Her warm mouth wasn't a finger's width away, but he pro-longed the moment by drawing a finger down her cheek.

He sat back abruptly, his heart pounding.

He'd done this before. The memory seared across his soul, leaving him yearning for more, yet breathless with fear.

The doctors were wrong. They said that after this long, the

chances of him regaining his memories were next to nil, but he'd refused to accept their prognosis. Knowing it would take something drastic to help him, he'd moved back to Memphis.

Well, he was here, and he'd evidently found what he came to find. So what the hell was he supposed to do now?

Emma woke suddenly, feeling sick and disoriented.

Her eyes flew open. Where was she? Why was she lying on a couch staring up a strange wall, at a ceiling she didn't recognize?

She turned her head, and memory flooded back.

Rafe. Was it really him? Here? Alive?

No, it couldn't be. Rafe died in Nicaragua six and half years ago.

The man who called himself David Johnson was bent over, picking something up, so his face was hidden. Then he straightened and placed her purse on the conference table, giving her his profile.

Her artist's eye recognized the details as if it was yesterday that she'd studied him out of love and a need to draw his dark, handsome face. The slight bump at the top of his nose that gave him a predatory look. The utter straightness of his coal-black hair. The square jaw.

How could he be here? How was it possible? Rafe was dead. Blown to pieces in a helicopter crash in God-knows-where Nicaragua. She'd seen the headlines. She'd talked to his parents.

"Rafe?"

Though she'd whispered the word, his head shot up, and he turned to face her, his dark eyes unreadable. "Yes?"

His response left no doubt. It was him.

"But...you're dead." She shook her head, but it didn't clear away his image. He was as solid as ever. "I must be dreaming."

"No." He took a limping step toward her. "You fainted."

Emma slowly pushed herself to a sitting position. She felt as if she weighed a ton. The hand she pressed against her spinning head felt cold, clammy. "I don't understand."

"I don't, either. You walked in, said my name, then passed out." He stepped closer and asked, "Are you all right?"

All right? She was hallucinating that her dead husband was standing right in front of her. "How could you be here?"

He gave her an odd look, then said, "I'm here to take over as editor and publisher for *Southern Yesteryears.*"

"Now I know I'm dreaming. You were never interested in the past."

"I wasn't?"

"That's one reason you were such a good reporter. You didn't care about yesterday's news. The only thing that mattered to you was what was happening now."

Confusion filled his eyes. "You came here for a job designing *Southern Yesteryears,* didn't you?"

"Well, yes, but—" She shook her head to clear her fuzzy brain of confusion. The action didn't help. "That's not what I asked you. How is it possible you're here? The *Commercial Appeal* said you died in a helicopter crash in Nicaragua."

He nodded jerkily, his face tight. "I did, for all practical purposes."

He was talking in circles.

"What does that mean?" she asked.

He stared at her for a long moment, then sat in the chair next to the couch. "Who are you?"

She blinked. "Who am I? You know perfectly well who I am. I'm Emma Lockwood. Emma Gr—"

"I know your name," he said impatiently. "How do you know me?"

"How do I know you?" She studied his dark, unreadable face. Red flags waved in her head like tree limbs in a violent thunderstorm. She suddenly remembered that Rafe had always answered questions with questions when he had something to hide or wanted to avoid a conversation. "What kind of game are you playing?"

"This is no game, I assure you. Please tell me who you are."

More confused than ever, Emma stared at him. What was he trying to pull? Why would he disappear for six and a half years, then suddenly show up, acting as if he didn't know her?

Unless...

She remembered her father snidely suggesting Rafe had faked his death to escape marriage.

It's how those half-breeds operate, her father had told her.

Emma had bitterly defended Rafe against her father's incredulous accusations. There'd been no doubt in her mind that Rafe had loved her.

Now... What else could it be?

She clenched her eyes. She couldn't think straight. Her mind still couldn't comprehend the fact that he was sitting here talking to her, much less figure out how or why.

Her eyes opened. Only Rafe could answer those questions. "Where have you been for the past six and a half years?"

He hesitated, then in a low, tight voice, answered, "In hell. How about you?"

Another question for a question.

Emma's heart disintegrated, leaving an aching, yawning hole in her chest. "My father was right, wasn't he? You left me."

He leaned back, the surprise on his face answering her accusation.

Her entire body went numb. She couldn't breathe, couldn't feel her heartbeat, couldn't even blink. She felt the way she'd felt the day she learned he'd died. Like her whole world had suddenly blown apart.

"Why did you come back? Did you think I still lived in Nashville? Or had Memphis grown so big you thought you wouldn't run into me?"

"I don't know what you're—"

"You left me. Alone. Do you know what my father put me through?" Hot tears stung her eyes. She rapidly blinked them away. "Of course you do. You knew exactly what he'd do when he found out. You just didn't care, did you?"

"Of course I...I mean I don't—" He plowed his hands back through his hair. "This is so sudden. I don't know what—"

"Sudden?" she cried. "You call six and a half years sudden?"

"Calm down. Please. I just want to—"

"To hell with what you want." If she sat there another second she'd either scratch his eyes out or start bawling. She didn't know which would be worse. To avoid either, she stood. Evading the hand he reached out to stop her, she walked to the door on legs so numb she could barely feel them.

He rose from the chair. "Please listen—"

"Listen to what? You're not saying anything." Feeling his ring roll against her heaving chest, she stopped and snatched it from under her blouse. "I don't need this anymore."

The ring hit him solidly in the chest. He caught it against his shirt, but the broken chain slithered to the floor.

Emma watched it pool on the blue industrial grade carpet. The last thing she had left to believe in. Gone.

"Please let me explain." He took a step toward her. "This isn't something I broadcast, but...I have amnesia. I don't know who you are."

"Amnesia?" She hesitated. Could it be true?

She wanted desperately to believe him, to believe he hadn't deserted her, to believe in the love she'd clung to like a lifeline all these years.

She studied his dark, earnest face, still so handsome it took her breath away. She wanted to trace the scar that marred his left cheek. She ached to taste his lips again. It had been so long since she'd felt strong, loving arms around her. She'd been so lonely.

But amnesia? That story had more holes than a spaghetti strainer. The largest being why didn't he or his parents call her when they found him? She'd talked to his mother several times, begged Mrs. Johnson to call if there was any word. True, she hadn't told his mother they were married. She'd thought the woman had enough to deal with. But she'd made it perfectly clear she was a good friend of Rafe's and cared what happened to him. Mrs. Johnson had assured Emma she would call if they learned anything, but she never did.

The only conclusion Emma could come to was that Rafe must've told her not to call. So it all came back to the glaring fact that he didn't want her. He even used his middle name now, probably hoping she wouldn't recognize it. He hadn't counted on her answering his ad.

She wished like hell she hadn't.

"I may have been born at night, but not last night." Her voice sounded tired, sad. Her movements were wooden as she took her purse from the table and pulled open the door. "Goodbye, Rafe."

Rafe sank back onto the chair. She didn't believe him.

He laughed mirthlessly. How could he expect her to? Amnesia was a story line from one of those sleazy tabloids they sell at grocery checkout stands. That's what he was—a damned sideshow.

He'd evidently left her in the lurch when he went on assignment. They must've been dating.

He lifted the ring she'd hurled at him. It was still warm from being nestled between her breasts. The thought caused a flash of heat to sear deep into his flesh. The reaction surprised him. He hadn't even thought about wanting a woman since he'd awakened in the nearest thing to hell there was on Earth. Why bother? No woman would want him, not after they saw his body.

Shoving aside the unwanted, unsatisfiable desire, he examined the ring. It was a gold class ring from the University of Texas. The date was eleven years ago. He twisted it in the light to read the initials inscribed inside.

He stood on a podium, in cap and gown, approaching the president of the university. As he reached for his diploma, the ring his mother insisted on buying for him glinted in the spotlights.

Startled by the sudden flash of memory, he dropped the ring.

They popped up so unexpectedly, from out of nowhere. Like shooting stars.

Was that how memories worked? He'd thought you controlled your memories, recalling them at will.

Breathing deep to settle his suddenly rapid pulse, he waited, but nothing else came. So much for control.

He picked the ring up and focused again on the initials inside. RDJ. Raphael David Johnson. Since he knew he'd attended the University of Texas from the diploma hanging on the den wall at home, he knew both the memory and the ring were his.

Why did Emma Lockwood have it? It was the kind of ring high school kids used to go steady. Is that what she'd been to him? A steady girlfriend? He'd only lived in Memphis six months when he got the job at the *Denver Post,* having worked his way up the reporting ladder in the Scripps-Howard chain. Was that enough time for him to become serious about a woman? Had they been engaged? This wasn't exactly an engagement ring. And he knew he'd had enough money in the bank to buy her a diamond, if that had been the case.

Damn.

He rested an elbow on one knee to support his aching head.

What the hell was he supposed to do now? This was why he'd come to Memphis, to find out about his past. Emma Lockwood seemed to hold the key, but he doubted she'd even come to the phone if he called, and a phone number was all he had for her.

Then his eye caught on a black corner peeking out from under the table. Standing, he slipped the ring into his shirt pocket and walked over to pull out a slim leather case. Her portfolio.

Curious, he unzipped it and spread her work on the table. Then smiled.

She was good. So good, he'd have hired her on the spot. This was the graphic artist he needed for *Southern Yesteryears.*

He pulled out an ad she'd created for an old-fashioned doll. This was exactly the look he wanted for his publication—something that appealed to women. In fact, this was the kind of ad he saw running in the refurbished, commercialized magazine he'd created in his head.

Then he spied a small piece of paper attached to the inside of the case. Her personal business card, complete with address and phone numbers.

Now he could find her. He needed Emma Lockwood—for himself and *Southern Yesteryears*.

She had the power to save them both.

Chapter Two

Emma killed the engine of her four-year-old Saturn and looked around blankly. She was home, parked in her usual spot in the protection of the carriage house that now served as their garage. Though she'd driven clear across town, her mind was in such upheaval she didn't remember a single mile.

The only thought she could hold on to, the only fact that mattered, was Rafe betrayed her—far worse than she'd ever believed.

It had been a betrayal of sorts, his dying. But at least he couldn't have helped that. No one chose to die. This...

This was a conscious act.

Her hands closed like a vise around the steering wheel when she remembered how stalwartly she'd defended him. After he'd "died," she'd stood up to her father for a whole month, enduring Cecil Grey's verbal and sometimes physical abuse.

Only after she'd been certain Rafe wasn't coming back—when the search for his body had been officially called off—did she give in to her father's orders to marry the man he'd handpicked for her from among Memphis's elite society. At that point, she'd have done anything to escape.

She'd endured almost two years of trying to fit herself into Jerry's life in Nashville. The first time he slapped her, however, she left. She wasn't going to put up with physical abuse from anyone anymore. She returned to Memphis, but since her father was just an older version of Jerry, she didn't move back home until her father died.

All this time, despite all she'd gone through, she'd believed Rafe had loved her. Her certainty was the only thing that sustained her when hope of seeing him again was gone; through the dark days married to a man she didn't love; when her father tried to force her back into the arms of an abusive husband.

Little by little, her faith in the goodness of life had been destroyed, until all she had to cling to was her trust in Rafe's love.

Now even that was gone. The last thing she had left to believe in had been shattered as completely as her heart had been, six and a half years ago.

What was she going to do now? How could she pretend her life hadn't been turned upside down and inside out? How was she going to get through each day?

"Mom!"

Emma blinked as a small ball of energy flew around the back of the car and skidded to a halt beside it.

"You're home early! Did you get the job? Can I stay up and watch the Braves game? It's on channel three instead of cable. Randy gets to watch. Can I, too, please? Huh? Can I?"

With a tired smile, Emma opened the door and drew her five-year-old son into her arms. Her self-pitying questions had been answered quickly. Gabe was her walking, talking, running, throwing reason for living. Having him made her look forward to getting up every morning.

He suffered her embrace for a moment, then wriggled away. Looking at her quizzically, he asked, "You been crying?"

With a frown, Emma swiped at the tear tracks on her cheeks. Never once had she let him see her cry. "I was...I had to drive into the sun, and it hurt my eyes."

Technically it wasn't a lie. The sun, intensified by tears, *had* hurt her eyes as she drove home.

Luckily her son's one-track mind accepted her explanation. "Can I stay up, Mom? The Braves game is on our TV! Can I, Mom? Please?"

Ever since Randy went to an Atlanta Braves game last summer, the boys had been die-hard Braves fans. Gabe only got to see his team play at Randy's house because most of the Atlanta games were on cable. Cable television was one expense their household did without.

"Randy gets to," Gabe argued.

Randy Jenkins was Gabe's best friend, by virtue of the facts that they were the same age, that Randy lived two doors down and that Emma's mother took care of him on weekdays while his parents worked, like she took care of Gabe. Randy's father was a research doctor at St. Jude Children's Hospital, and his mother was an assistant prosecutor for the city. They could afford cable. They could afford anything. It was impossible to compete with their money, so Emma didn't even try.

"What did Gams say?" she asked her son. Gams was the name Gabe had bestowed on his grandmother when he first started talking.

"She said I had to ask you."

No wonder he'd come tearing around the house like a tiny tornado. Emma hesitated. On one hand, she wasn't up to dealing with Gabe's excess energy for several extra hours tonight. On the other, she knew she wouldn't have to. If they let him chase fireflies until dark, gave him a warm bath, then settled down with him in front of the TV, he'd be asleep before the first commercial. "Okay, I guess. Is Gams on the back porch?"

Gabe nodded, then gave her an enthusiastic hug. "Thanks, Mom!"

She soothed her conscience by promising herself she'd record the game for him. They did have a VCR, several years old but still running.

"Did you get the job?" her son asked eagerly.

Emma shook her head. "No."

His face fell. "That means I don't get my own room."

"Not for a while. I'm sorry."

The roof had gotten so bad they'd had to abandon the second floor of the house altogether. They lived entirely on the first, which meant Gabe had to sleep with her in what was once the front parlor.

On the plus side, not having to air-condition the top floor cut their utility bill considerably.

Emma smoothed a lock of hair back from Gabe's forehead. "Go tell Gams I'll be there in a minute, okay?"

"Okay, Mom." Gabe ran out of the garage. Her son didn't walk anywhere. He zoomed.

With a sigh, Emma turned to grab her purse. Her hand paused over the well-worn leather. Something was missing. Her portfolio. Where—

With a groan she leaned her head on the steering wheel. She'd left it in the conference room at the motel. She'd been so upset when she left she didn't even remember she'd brought it.

What would Rafe think about her work? Would he bother to open it? Would he even see the thin, black leather case? It must've fallen under the table when she dropped it, or she'd have stepped on it on her way out.

She'd call the motel tomorrow, to see if someone had turned it in. The samples inside the case could be replaced. She'd taken them from the files of jobs she'd done for Harrison Printing over the last four years. But the portfolio itself was an expensive one. Her mother had given it to her for Christmas her first year as a graphic arts student at the University of Memphis. She'd hate to lose it.

The possibility that Rafe would return it popped into her mind, making her breath catch, but she quickly dismissed the notion. He hadn't bothered to contact her for six and a half years.

If he didn't care about his own son enough to call, he certainly wasn't going to bother with her old portfolio.

A few minutes later Emma stepped onto the screened back porch. Her mother sat in her favorite rocking chair in the shadows that were deepening in the twilight.

Emma laid her purse on a wicker table and sat in the cushioned chair beside it. "Gabe's still going strong, I see."

"He's already caught twenty-two lightning bugs in that bug box of his." Sylvia Grey smiled. "I've heard about every single one."

A whoop of triumph came from her son who ran toward the porch, holding his bug box aloft. "Twenty-three!"

"We're stopping at twenty-five, okay?" Emma called. "It's time for your bath."

"Awww, Mom."

"Twenty-five or fifteen minutes, whichever comes first. You want to watch the game, don't you?"

"Oh, yeah. Okay." He chased after another bug.

"Gabe said you didn't get the job," her mother said quietly.

"No, I didn't."

"How can you know so quickly? Did the man already hire someone?"

"No. I don't know. I mean..." Emma took a deep breath. "You'll never guess who I ran into at the interview. Never in a million years."

Obviously sensing her agitation, her mother threw a worried glance her way. "Who?"

"Rafe."

The name hung between them on the humid June air, like a mosquito looking for its next source of blood.

Finally her mother said, "Surely you don't mean *your* Rafe."

"*My* Rafe?" Emma laughed bitterly. "No. He's certainly not *my* Rafe."

Sylvia stopped the rocking motion of her chair, a sure sign of her distress. "How is that possible? He's dead."

"Apparently not." Emma shrugged, but the gesture felt far from nonchalant. "I guess Dad was right. I guess..." She paused to keep her voice from cracking. "I guess he didn't want me. Or Gabe."

"What do you mean? Do you think he faked his death?"

Emma shook her head. "That's what I thought at first. I was so shocked to see him. But I don't see how it's possible. I know he was hurt. He has an ugly scar on his face and his hand. Maybe he wasn't found until after I married Jerry, and he took that as an excuse to be rid of me."

"What did he say when he saw you?"

"He acted like he didn't know who I was. He said he has amnesia."

"Maybe he does." Sylvia started rocking again. "It happens all the time."

Emma rolled her eyes. "Only on those soap operas you watch."

"But, honey. It's possible for him to—"

"Mom, I called his mother several times during those weeks when he was missing. She knew I was concerned. Why wouldn't she have called me when they found him, unless he told her not to?"

Her mother's lips pressed together, which meant something had occurred to her that she'd rather not discuss.

"What is it, Mom?"

Sylvia sighed. "It's possible she did call. You would've moved to Nashville by then. If your father answered the phone..."

"He never would've told me or you, either," Emma said thoughtfully.

She leaned her head back against the wicker chair. Her brain ached from all the thinking she'd done since she'd walked into that conference room. Speculation, all of it. Rafe was the only one who could answer her questions, and he refused to explain anything. That alone told her she'd come to the right conclusions.

"Let's just drop it, okay? He obviously doesn't want anything to do with us, which is fine by me. I just thought you should know in case... Well, I was so upset, I left my portfolio there. He might try to return it, though I doubt it."

"Twenty-four!" Gabe cried.

After a moment of watching the boy chase tiny flashing lights, Sylvia said, "He *is* your Rafe. If he's not dead, you're still married to him."

Emma's jaw dropped, and she looked at her mother in horror. "What?"

"You were legally married, and you didn't get a divorce," her mother pointed out. "You're still married."

"But...I didn't...Jerry..." She groaned. "You're right. Damn."

Appalled by this latest complication, she ignored her mother's tongue clucking at the profanity. "It also means my marriage to Jerry wasn't legal. It probably wasn't, anyway, since Dad made me lie to the marriage license bureau when they asked if I'd been married before. What a mess." Emma closed her eyes and let her head loll against the chair. "What the heck am I going to do?"

"What can you do, honey?" her mother asked softly.

"Nothing." Emma straightened, her strength returning with her decision. "I can't do anything about it, and that's exactly what I'm going to do. Nobody's cared for the past six years. If we just leave things alone, chances are real good it'll never come up."

"What if you want to get married again? You're still young and—"

"No," Emma said firmly. "I don't need a man in my life, and I certainly don't want one. I've told you that."

"But, Emma, honey—"

"I mean it, Mom. Never again will I let a man have control

over me or my son. Men take over your life, like the Borg on *Star Trek*.''

Her mother gave her a blank look.

''I know you don't watch it, but trust me. It's exactly the same. I should know. I've been there, done that. No way am I buying the T-shirt.''

A car parked at the curb was odd enough on their street, but a shiny red truck with a Texas license plate made Emma's heart skip a beat as she turned into the driveway.

She pulled into the garage and shut off the engine, trying to convince herself it couldn't be Rafe. He used to drive fast, fancy sports cars—although red *was* his favorite color. But Rafe wouldn't hang around, even if he did show up. She'd seen the panicked look in his eyes.

This was probably an old friend of her mother's. Sylvia's grandfather and father had made their money in cotton, so she knew people from all over the South. Lots of cotton grew in Texas.

Emma tried to tell herself she was satisfied with the explanation, but when she entered the cool quiet of the house and heard the same deep, gravelly voice she'd been hearing in her dreams for the past two nights, she wasn't really surprised. However, that didn't keep her heart from pounding a jungle beat on her ribs.

Though she'd told herself over and over that he wouldn't come, she really knew all along that he would. The Rafe she'd known had been proactive. He met life head-on instead of just letting it happen. Whatever his excuse for not showing up the past six and a half years he wouldn't stand by and wait to see what she'd do, now that she'd discovered his deceit.

But whatever his excuse, she didn't want to hear it. After all these years, she had absolutely no interest in him or anything he had to say—on any subject.

Forcing herself to be calm, she closed the back door and laid her purse on the antique chest in the hall. Glancing at herself in the mirror above it, she caught herself running her fingers through her hair. She stopped as soon as she realized what she was doing, berating herself for wanting to look good.

Taking a deep breath, she entered the old "smoking parlor" that now served as their living room, then spied her son in the dining room next to it. Rafe sidled into view an instant later, his back to her, obviously helping Gabe set the table. Her son's face was animated as he asked Rafe a question about baseball.

Panic rose like bile in her throat as a brand-new horror occurred to her. What if Rafe was here to take away her son?

She rushed into the dining room. "What are you doing here?"

His head shot up, and the smile that had lit his dark face vanished. He stood at one end of the table, his hands gripping the back of the chair.

Oblivious to the tension between the adults in the room, Gabe ran around the table and threw his arms around her. "Hi, Mom. Guess what? Mr. Johnson's staying for supper. Gams made pot roast and—"

"What?" Emma straightened from hugging her son and turned to Rafe. "You can't stay."

Rafe watched her warily. "I came to return your portfolio and Sylvia was kind enough to invite me to supper. How could I refuse?"

"Simple. You open your mouth and say, 'No, thanks.'"

Gabe tugged on her skirt. "What's wrong, Mom? Don't you like him?"

She glanced down at her son, then back at Rafe. He had the nerve to quirk an eyebrow at her. How dare he question her behavior? Leaving a young, pregnant wife alone wouldn't exactly receive kudos from Miss Manners. "Why don't you go into the kitchen and help Gams, Gabe? Mr. Johnson and I need to talk."

Gabe looked between them, clearly worried. "He promised to play catch with me after supper."

And he promised to love me until death do us part, she wanted to tell her son. *See how much his promises are worth?*

"Go on now." She gave him a gentle push toward the kitchen door. "I'll call you when we're through."

"Is Mr. Johnson staying?" Gabe persisted, dragging his feet.

Emma said, "No," at the same time Rafe said, "Yes."

They looked at each other. Emma's gaze was intentionally sharp. Rafe's was determined.

Her eyes narrowed. She knew that implacable look. It meant he wasn't backing down from anything.

She hadn't remembered details like this in years. She wished she didn't remember them now.

Rafe was the first to look away. "I wouldn't be so rude as to back out on a dinner invitation once I've accepted it," he told Gabe. "Please tell your grandmother I'm staying if the offer still stands."

"It does."

They turned as one to see Mrs. Grey holding open the swinging door to the kitchen.

"Mother!" Emma took a step towards her. "What in the world possessed you to—"

"I invited a nice young man to dinner," Sylvia cut in sharply. "Can I not do that in my own house?"

"But he—"

"I taught you better manners than this, Emeline Katherine Grey *Johnson.*"

Chapter Three

Emma gasped. All color drained from her face.

Rafe stared at Sylvia in shock. Surely he hadn't heard...

But he had. Sylvia called her daughter Emma *Johnson*. What the hell...?

His stomach felt as if it were performing somersaults, and he had a sudden urge to run.

Gabe tugged at his grandmother's apron. "That's not Mom's name, Gams. Her last name's Lockwood, like mine."

Sylvia placed her hands on Gabe's shoulders and pushed him into the kitchen. "Come on, honey. Your mom and Rafe have some talking to do."

Rafe stared across the expanse of the mahogany table, clenching his hands, as if willpower alone could keep his stomach in place. "What did she mean?"

"Nothing. She's just getting a little senile." Avoiding eye contact, Emma walked around the table and headed for the kitchen.

Rafe cut off her escape, seizing her wrist to hold her. "At fifty-two—"

They faced each other in the middle of a shabby living room, but Rafe didn't care what it looked like. He had eyes only for Emma.

She wore a red velvet gown that made her cheeks glow. Holly sprigs decorated the headband holding back her long, blond hair.

The scent of a fresh-cut pine tree perfumed the air, mingling with the light floral fragrance she wore. The slender hands he held in his were trembling and cold. Her smile was nervous.

He wanted to drop a kiss on her lips to assure her everything was going to be all right. He would take care of her as long as he lived.

"Do you, Rafe Johnson, take Emma Grey to be your lawfully wedded wife? To have and hold from this day forward, for better, for worse, for richer, for poorer, in sickness and in health, forsaking all others, as long as you both shall live?"

"Yes, I most certainly do."

Rafe gasped and dropped her wrist like a line of hot type. His eyes focused on hers. "We were married."

Emma backed away, rubbing her wrist. "Now there's a news flash. Not exactly hot off the press, but who's quibbling?"

Rafe felt as if he were falling down a chasm with no light and no bottom. Married? For six years? Without knowing? How was that possible?

Panic rose in his throat. When he'd come to Memphis, he'd wanted to find his memories, but he'd never bargained for something like this.

"About to bolt again, aren't you? Fine. There's the door."

Rafe wanted to jump in his truck and get the hell out of there, to hide from this newest revelation like an ostrich burying its head in the sand.

But he couldn't. He'd spent the past year hiding from life, safe within the protection of his family, rarely venturing outside his parents' home for fear of what and who he might come across. During that time, he'd learned that, like the ostrich, hiding doesn't make life go away.

No, he couldn't run away now. Not when he'd found what he'd been looking for—in spades.

"I'm not the one who bolted the other night," he reminded her quietly.

She tore her gaze away with a huff.

"Give me a minute, all right? Being married may not be news to you, but it is to me."

"Oh, that's right. You have amnesia, don't you?"

He ignored both her question and the sarcasm with which it was delivered. Instead, he repeated the phrase he couldn't quite comprehend. "We were married. How is that possible?"

"We went to a justice of the peace in Mississippi and said 'I do.'"

"That's not what I said."

She glanced at him sharply. "Of course it is. What do you—"

"I said, 'Yes, I most certainly do.'"

Her eyes widened. "I'd forgot—" She crossed her arms over her stomach. "That doesn't prove anything."

"You'd forgotten. Why is it so impossible I had, too, until just now?"

"Forgetting tiny details is a long way from amnesia."

He threw his hands in the air. "What do you think? That I deserted you?"

"What else can I think?"

"That I just might be telling the truth about the amnesia?"

She lifted her chin.

He stared at the lovely woman standing a few feet away. Six years ago, he had married her. How could he have forgotten? Why didn't his—

At a sudden realization, he sucked in a breath. "We're still married. That's why your mother called you—"

"Shhh!" Emma leaped at him, shoving her hand over his mouth.

Rafe braced himself, but no memory surfaced. His only awareness was her cool hand on his face, her wide frightened eyes pleading with his. Had the magic ended? Or were the emotions coursing through both of them stronger than memory?

Or was magic of another kind messing with his mind? The kind of magic that could only be satisfied by burying himself deep in—

"We can't talk about this here," she whispered. "My son is right on the other side of that door."

He shook off his errant fantasies and her hand with them. "Then pick a place where we can speak freely. I'm not leaving until I get some answers."

For a minute she looked as if she wanted to refuse. He squared his shoulders, preparing to stand his ground, but suddenly she spun away.

"Come on, then. Let's get this over so you can leave." She didn't pause until she reached the entry hall. "Do you want to go upstairs or outside? It's going to be hot either way. We don't air-condition the second floor."

"I know. Sylvia and Gabe gave me a tour of the house this afternoon. Will Gabe be able to hear us if we go upstairs?"

She raised a pale eyebrow. "Depends on how much yelling you intend to do."

"As much as it takes." He waved for her to precede him. "At least there won't be any mosquitoes up there."

Emma ran up the stairs. With a foot on the first step, Rafe glanced up—and forgot to breathe. The tight muscles in her bottom were outlined clearly against the knee-length straight skirt. First one side, then the other, working to lift her up the—

With a soft curse, Rafe deliberately looked away. He'd never had these kinds of heated thoughts about a woman—at least not that he could remember.

He took a deep breath, then climbed slowly, both to give himself time to get his libido under control and so his bum leg wouldn't buckle.

When he reached the top, his leg had held up, but his heart was still in overdrive.

She waited for him in the upper hall. Glancing at his leg, she said with obvious reluctance, "It would've been easier for you if we'd gone on the front porch."

Could this be concern? For him? At least she blamed his heavy breathing on the climb.

He shrugged. "The doctors tell me I need to climb stairs more. It's supposed to stretch the tendons they had to shorten, one of the many times I was in the operating room."

She pressed her lips together, as if holding in something she didn't want to say. He'd seen the same expression on Sylvia's face several times this afternoon. Like mother, like daughter.

"Which room?" he asked.

She turned into the back one on the right. "In here. I have some things to give you."

Surprised and curious, he followed.

She switched on the overhead light, which also activated a ceiling fan, then disappeared into a closet on the other side of a shallow brick fireplace.

He knew this had been Emma's room, from the tour that afternoon. The only furniture that hadn't been moved downstairs was a desk, a chest and two nightstands, all of it pushed into the far corner and covered with heavy plastic. Three buckets sat on the floor, each on hardwood planks atop a square of plastic.

A moldy, musty smell permeated the room, even though the buckets were dry. Rafe ran his hand along the wooden mantel of the shallow coal fireplace. It was a cool contrast to the stifling air of the room and, amazingly, wasn't dusty. The upstairs rooms might be abandoned, but they were kept clean.

Rafe knew from Sylvia that the roof leaked. She'd also told him that was why Emma needed another job. Maybe she needed one bad enough to take the one he still planned to offer her.

"Come here and help me, will you?" she called from the closet.

He walked over to where Emma pulled at a large box sitting on the top shelf. Standing on tiptoe, she could barely reach the bottom. He entered and caught the corner of the box. As he did, his hand brushed hers.

He sat on the edge of her pink, ruffled bedspread, pushing damp hair off her face. Emma lay under the covers, her pale face totally devoid of makeup and her nose bright red.

"I need to be going," he told her. "Your parents will be home soon."

"Daddy will throw a holy fit if he finds you here." She caressed his wrist. "But I'm glad you came."

"How glad?" he murmured, lowering his head.

With a stiff arm, she held him away. "I told you, no kissing! I don't want to give you my cold."

Rafe dropped his arms and turned to her. She stood scant inches away, so close he could smell the light floral fragrance from his memories. "I've been in your room before."

She watched him dubiously. "So?"

"When we touched just now, I remembered one night when I must've sneaked into your house. You had a cold. Your parents had gone out. You told me your father would throw a holy fit if he caught me here, then I tried to kiss you, but you wouldn't let me. You didn't want to give me your cold."

Her green eyes widened to their absolute limits. "I'd forgotten about that time. I just remembered those two times we—"

"The times we what?" he demanded when she bit off her words.

She shivered, then tore her eyes away and ducked around him. "Just get down the box."

He sighed, then took a moment to calm his racing heart. Reaching for the box, he carried it into the room. "What's in it?"

She faced one of the windows looking out over the backyard, her arms crossed so far over her stomach he could see her fingers grasping her slender waist. "It's the things you left. When you died—or we thought you did—I went to your apartment and cleaned it out. There wasn't much. Mostly clothes, which I gave away. You'd rented your furniture.''

He set the box on the plastic-covered desk, then took out his keys to break the tape. ''I never even thought about the things I left in Memphis. My parents apparently didn't, either.''

''The landlord called me because he knew me, I was over there so much. I thought about sending everything to your parents, but...'' She drifted off as if she'd forgotten what she was going to say. Turning, she studied his face for a long moment. ''You said in the closet that when you touched me, you remembered the night I had a cold. What did you mean?''

Was she finally starting to believe him? He barely restrained a sigh of relief, which told him how important her trust was to him. How could that be? He barely knew this woman.

He barely knew his own wife.

Shaking away his confusion, he locked his gaze onto hers. ''You give me back my memories.''

Her eyes widened. ''What?''

''When you fainted at the motel and I picked you up, I remembered something from my life before the accident. You can't possibly know how remarkable that is. For over six years, I haven't been able to remember anything except what my family told me to remember. But those weren't real memories. They didn't have sights or smells or sounds.'' He pushed a hand through his hair. ''I've remembered something almost every time I've touched you.''

''No.'' Emma tightened her arms around herself to keep them from trembling. His words made it sound as if there was some primal connection between them that still existed. But it couldn't be true.

Rafe pulled out his wallet and withdrew a yellowed, stained piece of notebook paper with burned edges. He unfolded it with meticulous care, as if it were the Shroud of Turin.

Her heart skipped a beat. She knew what it was before she saw the picture she'd casually tossed off while daydreaming during a boring art history lecture at the university. She'd drawn Rafe as the archangel Raphael, the angel of healing. That very night Gabe had been conceived.

He stared down at the drawing. "When I caught you after you fainted, I remembered when you gave me this. We were standing by the Mississippi River." Rafe held the paper out to her. "You drew it, didn't you?"

She swallowed to clear the lump from her throat, but it popped right back up. So she nodded.

"They found this clutched in my hand when they rescued me," he said. "That's why it's so dirty and the edges are burned. It's a miracle it survived the blast. Probably the only reason is because my flesh took the punishment, protecting it. It's the only clue I had to my life during the months before my father found me. Some days it was the only thing that kept me sane."

Emma reached a trembling finger out to touch the paper. "I can't believe you still have it."

"What does EKG mean?"

She traced the letters in the heart she'd drawn on the angel's robe. "They were my initials before we got married. You used to..." Her voice cracked. "You used to make terrible puns comparing loving me to the medical test doctors do on heart patients."

He hesitated, then said, "So I loved you."

The past tense shot darts of pain into her heart, which startled her. Pain meant his words hurt, which meant she still cared. But she didn't. She couldn't. "Yes, of course."

"And you loved me?"

Not trusting her voice, she nodded.

"Then, beautiful Emma, for the sake of the love we once shared, won't you believe I'm telling the truth?"

Emma felt as if she were drowning. She'd trusted just three men in her life, and they'd all betrayed her in one way or another. One of them was standing here now, asking her to trust him again.

Even though it seemed as if he hadn't knowingly betrayed her, she couldn't erase the last six years. She didn't know why she had to.

"What do you want from me?" she asked.

He frowned, obviously disappointed that she'd avoided answering his question. "Several things. First and foremost, for you to believe I didn't leave you alone on purpose. You must've known me well, to have married me. Did I seem to be the kind of person who would desert his wife?"

"No," she had to admit. "You were the most honest, direct person I'd ever met. It was one of the main reasons I loved you."

His face softened, and he smiled for the first time. "Thank you."

Emma caught her breath. It was like looking into the face of an angel. A scarred angel with broken wings. She used to live for his smiles. "Thank you for what?"

"For believing me," he answered. "You do, don't you?"

Suddenly she realized she did, and it terrified her. Believing him was dangerous. It meant he would expect a place in her life, a place she didn't have to give him. "Just because I believe you have amnesia doesn't mean I trust you."

His smile faded, and sadness crept into his eyes. "At least it's a start. Maybe now you'll be willing to answer my questions."

She lifted her chin. "First you need to answer a few of mine."

"I'll tell you anything I know, which I assure you isn't much."

She ignored his feeble attempt at a joke. "Why wasn't I told when you were found?"

He blinked. "My parents knew we were married?"

"No, but—"

"Why not?"

She sighed and relaxed her iron grip on her stomach. "It was my fault. My father objected to me dating you—strenuously. I wouldn't let you tell your parents or anyone else we were dating, much less married. I was afraid my father would somehow find out."

"Were you ashamed of me?"

"No, of course not. My father..." She looked away, even now unable to denigrate the man who'd made her life so miserable. "Your mother was from Mexico, which made you a half-breed in his eyes. If he'd known I was dating you, he would've...not have been happy."

His eyes narrowed. "How...not happy?"

She shrugged. "He would've locked me in my room and probably...probably..."

"Hit you?"

She nodded.

Rafe released a soft Spanish curse.

Emma held her hand up to stop any more questions along that line. "It's in the past now. He's dead. But you knew what he was like. We dated in secret, and married in secret. You were about to go off on an assignment, your first for the *Denver Post*. We were planning to break the news to my parents as soon as you got back from Nicaragua, then we were going to drive to Houston for Christmas and tell yours, then move to Denver. We were so young. We didn't think a few days could matter."

He absorbed what she said, then asked, "If my parents didn't know about you, how can you have expected them to call when they found me?"

"I talked to your mother after the accident, several times. I told her I was a friend, and asked her to call me if they found anything. She said she would."

He lifted a dark brow. "A friend?"

She halfheartedly lifted her hands. "I didn't know how to tell them I was their daughter-in-law, married to the son they'd just lost. They had enough to deal with, and I thought they'd think I was some sick psycho, wanting money or something. It didn't seem to matter, since you were gone."

He frowned thoughtfully. "Now that you mention it, I do remember Mama saying something about not being able to reach a friend of mine in Memphis. She may have even said your name, but it wouldn't have meant anything to me. At that point, my own name didn't mean anything to me.''

"Speaking of names, why are you calling yourself David?''

He searched her eyes, his face bleak. Finally, he said, "Because Rafe was dead. It seemed only fitting that this new person should be called something new.''

Emma felt as if a giant hand was squeezing every last drop of blood from her heart. "Oh, Rafe.''

He regarded her with a mixture of awe and uncertainty. "I don't know why I told you that. I've never told anyone. I told my parents that David sounded more American than Raphael. I was starting to write for several history magazines and needed an all-American name.'' He paused, then said, "I think I believed it myself, for a while.''

"History,'' she murmured. "You were never interested in history.''

"Wasn't I? Well, when you have no history of your own, you tend to grab hold of any you can find.'' He smiled sadly. "My father has always been a Civil War buff, and he encouraged my interest. Plus, it was something I could research and write without dealing with people.''

She gave him a puzzled look. "You always liked people. You never met anybody you couldn't talk to.''

He nodded. "My family told me the same thing. I knew they worried about me when I wouldn't go out. But you see, people ask questions. They expect you to know them, to know about things that have been washed from your mind. It was—'' he looked away "—awkward.''

Tears burned her eyes. He'd suffered so much. So had she. She wanted to run to him and kiss away his hurt, her pain.

But she didn't. It wouldn't solve anything. It wouldn't erase their pain. Like he said, Rafe was dead. His mind, at least, if not his body. This was an entirely different man from the one she'd married—David Johnson, not Rafe.

She'd changed, too. They'd both lived several lifetimes during

the past six years. They could never go back. The young, innocent couple who believed they could set the world on fire was
gone. In their place were two damaged adults who were worlds
apart.

Still, she was glad he came. She'd needed closure, even though
closure brought more pain. "Thank you."

His brow lifted. "For what?"

She shrugged. "For coming. For explaining. It's helped a lot.
I'm glad you're not dead, Rafe. And I'm glad to know you didn't
desert me. I'm sorry I acted so badly before."

"I understand now. It's no wonder you thought what you did."

She stuck out her hand. "I wish you well. I really do."

He glanced at her hand, frowning. "You sound as if you're
saying goodbye."

"There isn't any point in dragging this out, is there? You have
your answers, and I have mine."

"No point in..." He lifted his hands in exasperation. "You've
forgotten one tiny detail, haven't you? We're married."

"No, I haven't forgotten." She retracted her hand. She
should've known he wouldn't let her off so easily. "But if you
think that means we're going to pick up where we left off,
you—"

"I have no idea where we left off!" He shoved a hand back
through his hair. "But I'm not going to let you dismiss me with
a handshake."

Again, her hands crossed over her stomach. "What do you
mean?"

Rafe studied her. Talk about body language. She'd drawn herself in like a turtle into its protective shell, and she stared out of
it as if she expected to be attacked any minute. What had she
gone through, this beautiful woman with haunted green eyes?

Suddenly and with keen desperation, he wanted to know. He
wanted to become the shell that protected her, the one she ran to
and hid inside when she was scared. He wanted to find out who
she was—inside and out—then start all over again.

The depth of the feeling amazed him. He'd been so wrapped up in his own troubles for so long that he hadn't had the time or energy to deal with anyone else's.

Why now? Why this woman? Was their connection from the past so strong it had called him back to Memphis?

Whatever they shared, it was strong enough to open the doors to his past that had been sealed for years. She was his angel of healing. Fate had brought them together again. He'd be damned if he'd let her go with, "Have a nice life."

"What do I mean?" he repeated softly. "I mean that I need you. You give me back my memories. You have to help me. You're the only one who can."

She slowly shook her head. "No."

"When I touch you, I remember. That hasn't happened since I woke up in that hellhole in Nicaragua."

"Don't say that."

His eyes narrowed. "Why not? It's true."

"Because it makes it seem like…like I'm important to you. Like there's some kind of connection between us. And there isn't. There can't be."

"How can you say that? What else drew me back to Memphis? What made you answer that ad?"

She threw her hands in the air. "Coincidence."

He shook his head. "It was fate, Emma. I didn't know why the need to return to Memphis was so strong. But now I do. Fate called me back so I could find you. Fate made you answer my ad."

Emma closed her eyes and pressed her lips together. She drew in a deep, ragged breath, then said, "It wasn't fate, Rafe. It was desperation." She opened her eyes. "I needed another job. I'm sorry, but I have too much to deal with in my own life to be any help to someone else. I don't have the time or the energy."

He lifted a brow. "You have time and energy for a second job."

"No, I don't. I hardly ever see my son now, only a few hours a day. If I get another job, I'll never see him. But I need money to fix the roof.''

She'd given him the perfect opening. He parted his lips to offer her the job, then abruptly closed them. What she said made an idea pop into his mind, and he turned to face the window as he considered it.

She needed a job, yet also needed to stay home. He needed a graphic artist and also an apartment/office. Why not rent a couple of these rooms for a few months? They weren't using them, and it would make his offer that much more attractive to her, if she could earn money at home. If he was around every day and every night, sooner or later she'd have to deal with him.

Now if he could only convince her to agree—or bribe her, or bully her. Whatever worked.

He glanced around thoughtfully. "How long have you been sleeping downstairs?"

She looked confused at the change of subject, but answered, "Two and a half months. I've been trying to find a job, but part-time graphics jobs at night are few and far between in this town."

"Funny you should mention needing a job. The main reason I came here today was to offer you the graphics job on *Southern Yesteryears*. After you left the other night, I looked over your portfolio. I liked what I saw. A lot. Right now, *Southern Yesteryears* isn't much more than a quarterly newsletter called *Southern History*. I've been writing freelance articles for it the past several years. When it came up for sale a month ago, I bought it and I moved here a couple of weeks ago. My goal is to make it into a real commercial magazine—as essential on Southern coffee tables as *Southern Living*. And as good."

Despite her determination to be rid of him, Emma was intrigued—and relieved their discussion about the past was over. "I don't know of any kind of publication like that. Odd that no one's thought of it, since most Southerners can recite their lineage back beyond the Civil War. But if you want to make it a success, you'll have to—"

She pressed her lips together. She shouldn't be this interested in a job she couldn't have. It would get her hopes up, and his.

"I'll have to what? Please, I want your input. I need all the help I can get if I'm going to make it a success." When she didn't reply, he continued, "That's why I need you. You're the best artist who answered my ad. You have a real flair for color and for making pages easy to read. I especially liked the ad you did for that old-fashioned doll. The one dressed in the green dress."

Emma liked the doll ad, too. It was some of her best work.

"That's the look I want for *Southern Yesteryears*," he said. "You're the artist I want. Please take the job."

She wanted to say yes. She didn't often have work as creative as that doll ad. Working for a printing company, the day-in, day-out work was mostly routine—stationery, brochures, business cards. To be the creative force behind a magazine comparable to *Southern Living* was something she'd only dreamed of doing. But because she didn't have the chance to finish her degree, she'd thought it was something forever beyond her grasp.

"How much does it pay?" she asked tentatively.

He named a monthly sum that would give her half again what she made at Harrison Printing. "But the best part about it is you can work right here at home."

That caught her attention. "What? How? I don't have a computer system of any kind, much less one that can handle something like this."

He hesitated, then dug a hand back through his hair again. It was a gesture she didn't remember him using before, one which spoke of constant frustration. "That brings me to the second part of my proposal." He took a deep breath. "I want to rent a couple of rooms."

She gasped and took a step back. "Here?"

He hurried on. "In exchange for six months' rent, I'll put a new roof on the house as soon as it can be arranged. I've been looking for a place to live and work. This would be perfect for me.''

''No!''

''Think of the advantages for you. The house would be fixed right away, so you'll avoid any more damage. You'll have a steady second income to make other repairs needed around here. You'll work at home, so you can spend time with your son. Get a second job somewhere else, and you'll never see him.''

Emma crossed her arms across her stomach. He certainly knew how to push her buttons. But then, he'd always been good at that. She supposed it was a skill he'd been born with, one he couldn't forget. ''Why would you want to rent these stuffy old rooms?''

''I can think of several advantages for me. Six months would give me time to learn the city again, to find out exactly where I want to locate the magazine's offices when it outgrows a one-room operation. Plus your mother is here almost all the time. I'm going to have to invest in some expensive computer equipment for you to use, and I'll be out of town now and then doing research and trying to secure advertisers. It'd be nice to have someone around to keep an eye on it.'' He ran a hand almost lovingly along the window frame. ''And what better place to start a magazine about history than in a house that has seen so much of it?''

''You mean you actually like this old firetrap?''

He glanced back at her in surprise. ''Of course. Don't you?''

She shook her head. ''The upkeep takes all of my time and money. I've tried to convince Momma that if we sold the house and most of the antiques, we'd have enough money to buy a brand-new house in one of the suburbs. Then Gabe could attend a decent school.''

''So why haven't you moved?''

Emma sighed. ''Every time I bring the subject up, Momma gets this hurt look on her face. She's lived in this old mausoleum all her life and doesn't want to part with a single lamp.''

His dark gaze bored into hers. "Sounds like you need this job even more than I thought."

Emma looked away. She knew she should take Rafe's offer. She wasn't likely to get another half as good. Not only would she have the money to fix the roof, but she'd be expanding her creativity doing something she loved. Who knew where a job like this could lead? Plus she'd be able to work at home so she could be with Gabe.

But how could she work with Rafe, much less let him live in her home? She needed to avoid him, not spend day after day in his company. Even though she was determined never to let a man in her life again, she recognized the first stirrings of attraction. It was probably just echoes of the love they'd once shared, which would die out when she got to know him.

But what if it wasn't? What if she fell in love with him again?

Every relationship she'd ever had with a man had brought her nothing but trouble and heartache. She couldn't put herself through that again. She just couldn't.

As well knowing they were married, he might start thinking he had rights, especially if they were living under the same roof.

The heat in the room grew oppressive as she remembered the "rights" he'd taken full advantage of during the single night of their honeymoon, and the times before that, one of which had gotten her pregnant. He'd been a thorough, thoughtful, passionate lover. She wondered if he still was.

Which was precisely why she had to avoid him.

She shook her head slowly. "I'm sorry, but I can't."

"Can't what? Can't rent the rooms or can't take the job?"

"Can't do either."

"What if I swear to keep our relationship all business?"

She shook her head again.

"Why?" he asked in frustration.

"Because you won't. And I don't just have myself to think about," she said softly. "I have to protect my son."

His black eyes burned like coal. "You think I'm going to hurt Gabe?"

Emma steeled herself. She'd hoped she could get rid of Rafe so she could think, so she wouldn't have to tell him—yet—about Gabe. She'd wanted to protect her son at least another day.

But now she had to tell him. She had to get it over with. Get everything in the open.

Maybe she'd get lucky. Learning he had a wife had scared him so much he'd nearly run away. Finding out he had a son might send him packing.

"You've already hurt him, by leaving him when he was inside of me. By going off on a dangerous assignment, even when I begged you not to go. Your work was more important to you than me." She blinked back the tears stinging her eyes. "More important than your child."

Rafe's dark face went white. "My...child?"

"He's yours, Rafe. Gabe is your son."

Chapter Four

Shock held Rafe motionless, as if he'd suddenly been encased in ice. Gabe was his?

"It can't be true," he said, his voice a raspy whisper.

Emma's eyes narrowed. "You only have to look at him to know he's yours. That was one thing my father didn't bargain on when he tried to pass Gabe off as Jerry's. Jerry's hair isn't much darker than mine. Nobody was fooled."

Rafe made a conscious effort to breathe, which made his heart kick into overdrive. He'd thought finding out about his past would give him control over his life. Instead, her words sent him hurling into outer space, more out of control than ever.

As the idea took hold, however, the wild careening transformed into joy like he'd never known. Suddenly he felt as if he were racing for the stars.

He had a wife and a son—a family—something he thought he'd never have. Now, in the space of four words, he had it all.

Gabe. Gabriel. She'd named him after another archangel.

He could see the resemblance now. The boy looked just like him in a picture his mother had shown him of himself at Gabe's age. Black hair, black eyes, a skinny body just beginning to catch up to the size of his head.

Why hadn't he seen it instantly? He'd been with Gabe for hours this afternoon. All that time he'd been talking to his son. His own flesh and blood. "I can't believe it..."

Emma's face tightened and she spun away from him. "Fine. Don't. We haven't needed you for the past almost-six years. We certainly don't need you now."

She'd reached the door before he realized she was leaving. "Wait!"

She paused with her hand on the knob but didn't look back. "What?"

"Was that why we got married?" he asked hesitantly.

She finally turned to face him. "It was why we married so quickly. We were planning to wait until you'd moved to Denver and found us a place to live. But when you learned I was pregnant, you refused to wait."

A million thoughts ran through his head, but he couldn't grab hold of a single one. She stood patiently by the door, watching him, her face unreadable.

"I can't believe—"

Her eyes narrowed, and she began to turn away.

He closed the gap between them, seizing her arm to keep her from leaving. "It's not that I don't believe he's my son. You're right. He looks too much like me to deny it. I just—" He rammed a hand back through his hair. "I feel like I've been hit with a ton of bricks."

"I felt the same way when I walked into that conference room the other night and saw you—" She glanced down at his hand on her arm. "You're touching me."

Though the tone of her voice didn't convey displeasure, the comment did. He released her immediately. "Sorry. I didn't mean—"

"I just wondered if you're remembering anything else."

He shook his head, relieved that she wasn't repulsed by his

touch. "It doesn't happen every time. I guess my mind has enough to deal with right now. It was the same when you covered my mouth downstairs, right after I learned we're married."

She nodded, and they fell silent.

Rafe studied her lovely face, memorizing the delicate features—of his wife. This woman had borne him a son, and he'd never even known. He'd never—

Suddenly his eyes narrowed. "My mother and father have had a grandson for nearly six years they don't know about? Why the hell didn't you tell them?"

"I told you I didn't know how. I was only nineteen. I'd never met your parents. I didn't know how they'd react."

He knew his parents wouldn't be satisfied with that explanation, but he had to remember the kind of father Emma had grown up with. Then again... "Sylvia isn't like your father. Why didn't she help you?"

"My mother is very old-fashioned. She never questioned my father's right to rule the household. I've been trying to cram some women's lib into her, but..." She lifted a hand helplessly. "It's the way she was raised."

He stared at her a long time, trying to work his way through the confusion, elation and anger. Finally, he asked, "What are we going to do?"

Her eyes widened. Surely it wasn't fear he saw in the green depths.

"Do?" she asked hesitantly. "About what?"

"About...everything you've told me."

It was as if a curtain dropped behind her eyes. "*We* are not going to do anything. I told you. We don't need you." She took a step back. "You'd better go. I'll make your excuses."

She disappeared through the door.

Rafe barely noticed.

We don't need you.

Her words rammed into his soul, striking at the very heart of his psyche, at the innermost fears he'd never admitted even to himself.

She didn't need him. No one needed him.

He hadn't realized until that moment what was missing from his life, besides memories. He wanted to be needed, to be as necessary to someone as ink was to newsprint.

Why hadn't he realized it before?

Probably because he'd been doing nothing but taking ever since his father rescued him from that muddy hole in Nicaragua. He'd taken his family's love, their help in healing his broken body, their support in returning to a life of his own.

It wasn't that he hadn't given anything back. He'd returned his family's love and would do anything for them—but what he had to give wasn't necessary to any of them. His parents had each other, his brothers and sisters all had their spouses and children of their own.

Rafe had been the odd man out, emotionally as well as physically.

Emma said she didn't need him, either, but he sure as hell needed her. For the first time since he'd wakened in the village, he felt a connection to someone, a link to the man he'd been.

But what did a man with a broken mind and a broken body have to give the beautiful woman who could lift the impenetrable curtain from his past? Only a lousy job. How could that compare to what he needed from her? To what she'd already given him?

Feeling as bereft as he'd felt all those months when he didn't even know his name, Rafe wandered over to the window. Placing his hands on either side, he leaned into them, staring blindly out at the sun dropping toward the treetops. Noise drew his eyes down to where Gabe played in the backyard, tossing a baseball into the air and catching it in his glove.

Pride swelled like a balloon in Rafe's chest. His son. From the time they'd spent together, he knew the boy was smart, inquisitive and loving.

Emma had done a good job raising Gabe—without him.

As he watched, Gabe dropped the ball. He'd have to show him how to spread the glove, so he'd have more—

Realizing what he was thinking, Rafe shook his head. He didn't have any right to—

He straightened away from the window.

The hell he didn't. He was Gabe's father. And whether she liked it or not, he was Emma's husband. Those two facts gave him all kinds of rights.

Besides, he did have something more to give than a lousy job. He'd played baseball all his life and had been on a winning team in college, according to his yearbook. He remembered enough about the sport to help his nephews. He could help his son, too— teach Gabe the finer points of the game.

Hell, there were lots of things he could teach his son. Things Emma couldn't. Like sportsmanship. How to bait a hook. How to avoid a fight, and how to end the fight quickly if he couldn't avoid it.

Gabe needed a father. Gabe needed him.

And though Rafe couldn't say how or why, something in his gut told him Emma needed him, too.

There was a sadness, a loneliness that never quite left her face. Maybe he had the power to erase it, to bring back the joy and love he'd seen shining in her marvelous green eyes in his memo—

Love? The word, and all it implied, caught in his mind.

Well, maybe not love. He wasn't the man he'd been when she'd loved him a lifetime ago. He couldn't expect her to love him again, scarred as he was. But he could help her. Monetarily, if nothing else. And maybe they could find a way to be friends.

The desire he'd felt for Emma from the moment she'd walked in the conference room door two days ago sprang up to mock him. How could he settle for friendship when all he wanted to do was hold her in his arms until she wasn't aware of anything but him, to kiss her wide, luscious mouth and see if the same sparks ignited that flew between them when they touched, to bury himself inside her and brand her as his?

He had to, that's all there was to it. She'd made it clear she didn't want a man in her life, but everyone needed a friend. If that was the only way she'd accept him, then so be it.

He'd do anything for her, and for his son.

"I see you sent Gabe out to play," Emma said as she entered the kitchen.

Sylvia turned. "Where's Rafe?"

"He's leaving."

"I didn't hear the front door," her mother said sharply.

Emma shrugged.

"What did you say to him?"

Emma took a deep breath. "I told him Gabe was his."

Sylvia nodded. "I expect he'll be down directly, then."

"No, he won't. I told him to leave."

"And you think that'll make him scurry off, do you?" Sylvia clucked her tongue. "You've been dealing with a five-year-old too long."

"What do you mean?"

"Once he's had time to mull things over, he'll come on down to take things in hand. About time we had a man around the house again. I—"

"Take things in hand?" Emma threw her own hands in the air. "That's exactly what I don't want."

"Now, honey, I know you think you don't need a man. But that's pure hurt talking. A woman needs a man around. It's nature's way."

Emma rolled her eyes. Her mother came from a generation that believed in one man and one woman for life. But that fairy tale had blown up in Emma's face too many times for her to believe in happily ever after. "The last time I checked we were living in the twentieth century, almost the twenty-first. Women have come a long way in the last fifty years. We have jobs now. We can support ourselves. Men are superfluous.''

Sylvia lifted a brow. ''Gabe came by immaculate conception, did he?''

''Okay, maybe men serve one purpose, but a woman who wants children would only need one around for a few minutes every few years. Even if I wanted more children, I couldn't afford them, so I don't have that problem.'' Emma crossed her arms over her stomach. ''Aren't we ready to eat yet? I'm starving.''

''Whenever Rafe comes down.''

Emma pressed her lips together to keep from screaming. What was with her mother? They'd gotten along so well ever since her father died, working together to raise Gabe and to keep the house from falling apart. Now Sylvia acted as if a man would solve all their problems. ''I told you, he's leaving. He's not eating with us.''

''If you're sure...''

''I'm sure.''

''Well, then, get the serving bowls down, will you, honey?''

Several silent minutes passed as they prepared the food for the table. Finally Sylvia asked, ''What about the job? Rafe told me he was going to offer it to you.''

Emma paused in her task of arranging the potatoes and carrots around the pot roast. ''He did.''

Her mother turned to her. ''And?''

''And nothing.'' Emma resumed her work. ''You fixed an awful lot of potatoes.''

''I thought we were having a guest. Men can eat a lot of potatoes. The job didn't pay enough?''

''The salary was fine.'' She should've known her mother wouldn't let it go.

''The hours weren't good?''

Emma placed the large spoon down with a thump and faced her mother. ''The hours were fine. They were perfect, as a matter of fact. The salary would give us half again what I'm making now. Plus he offered to fix the roof on top of everything.''

''Then what's the problem?''

''The problem...'' The irritation left as quickly as it had come. ''The problem is me. Rafe wants to rent a couple of rooms upstairs to live and work in, and I don't think I can stand having him around so much.''

''But that would be perfect,'' Sylvia exclaimed. ''You'd be working right here at home. You were afraid getting another job would take you away from Gabe all the time.''

''I know, but...''

''But what? How could you ask for a better opportunity?''

''I couldn't. It's perfect. Great money and great hours doing what I've always wanted to do—all in the comfort of my own home.'' Emma shook her head slowly. ''But he'd be living here, Momma. Day in. Day out. He'd be here all the time.''

''He should be living here, honey. He's your husband and Gabe's father.''

''Those are just technicalities.'' Emma flicked her hand, wishing she could wave her problems away as easily. ''He was my husband for all of fourteen hours before he left. He hasn't been around for six and a half years.''

''That's not his fault.''

''I know, but...'' Emma closed her eyes. She was so confused. ''How can I let him back in my life? He'll take over everything.''

Sylvia shrugged. ''So? Are you saying you wouldn't like a little more help around here? You're exhausted most of the time.''

''Help is one thing. Having to fit my life around his is something else entirely. That's what men expect you to do. I was supposed to quit school and move to Denver with Rafe because of his career. I moved to Nashville so Jerry could finish his law degree.'' She lifted a hand helplessly. ''I have to think of myself for once, and Gabe. I have my own career, which I don't want to give up.''

"Doesn't sound like he's asked you to give up anything."

"No, but he could. It's what men do."

Sylvia shook her head sadly. "You've loved Rafe for almost seven years. You wore his ring around your neck all this time. Did your love disappear because he showed up on your doorstep?"

Emma looked away. "This Rafe is an entirely different man from the one I loved. I don't know who he is anymore."

"Then get to know him again. One thing I can tell you from the time I spent with him today—he's not the kind of man who's going to give up easily. Look how long he's been searching for his memories. Do you think he's going to walk out of your life now, especially knowing Gabe is his son?" Sylvia patted her shoulder. "You're going to have to deal with him on some level."

"I know, I know. I just..." Emma sighed.

"You might as well get paid for—" Sylvia broke off at the distinct sound of uneven footsteps on the stairs.

Emma and Sylvia froze, listening. When the steps didn't disappear out the front door, but instead came down the hall, Emma caught her breath, while her mother gave her an "I told you so" look.

Seconds later, Rafe filled the doorway. His eyes sought hers immediately. In the dark depths she saw uncertainty and hope mixed with a strong dose of determination. She should've known he wouldn't meekly leave just because she told him to. Though she groaned inwardly, she recognized a tiny thrill of pure feminine satisfaction that he was determined to have a place in her life.

She immediately squelched the feeling.

"Can we talk?"

His raspy voice sent chills over her skin. "Rafe, I—"

"Surely you can wait," Sylvia said, a trifle too brightly. "We're about to put supper on the table."

"Momma, we don't need to—"

"To let this juicy pot roast dry out. Besides—" Sylvia looked at her pointedly "—you have some things you need to ponder awhile. The advantages of certain situations, remember? I figure the hour it'll take for supper will give you enough time."

Emma rolled her eyes at her mother's less-than-subtle statement.

Rafe cleared his throat. "Sylvia, Emma and I—"

"Can go out for coffee and dessert after supper." Her mother waved a hand toward the back door. "Call Gabe in, will you? And make sure he washes up."

Rafe met Emma's eyes again. With a rueful smile, he shrugged, telling her he recognized her mother's high-handed manner, but what could they do?

The silent communication broke through Emma's defenses as nothing else could. She couldn't help smiling back.

Rafe's face seemed to light up, making it seem as if his eyes caught fire. "After supper, then?"

She nodded, then quickly picked up the pot roast.

Supper was not the ordeal Emma had expected it to be. Rafe was as good at getting people to talk as he'd ever been, an important trait for a reporter. When he wasn't talking to Gabe about baseball, he was asking Sylvia about the antiques lining the walls of every room in the house.

Emma didn't say much, just watched him, marveling anew at the miracle—mixed though it was—of having him here, alive.

Both she and her mother were right. Emma had loved Rafe for so many years, it was impossible to turn off the feelings overnight. And even though she knew he wasn't the same man she'd loved six years ago, there were moments when that was hard to remember. His voice still made goose bumps dance over her skin; his gaze still trapped her breath in her lungs; his touch still made her knees feel like jelly.

Which wasn't good. The possibility of falling in love with him again frightened her so much she completely lost her appetite.

How could she let him move into her home, work with him day after day?

Yet the more she thought about his offer, the more she knew she had to take it. She'd be crazy not to, no matter how uncomfortable having him around would be.

She'd just have to protect her heart. She could do it if she insisted on keeping their relationship on a strictly business level. She worked with men every day at Harrison Printing and didn't fall in love with them. This shouldn't be any different.

At that moment, he met her gaze across the table. His face softened perceptibly, and he held her eyes a second longer than necessary.

When he finally looked away, air rushed into Emma's lungs with a whoosh. Okay, maybe this *would* be different. She didn't have a past with the men at work. Hadn't had a child with them. Keeping her wits about her would be harder, but she could do it. She just had to keep reminding herself of how men tended to take over women's lives. Maybe if she envisioned a Borg every time she looked at Rafe, it would help.

She spent several minutes trying with her artist's mind to make Rafe look like one of the evil creatures on *Star Trek*. The ones that took over entire civilizations, robbing people of their identities as they "assimilated" them into the Borg culture. She tried attaching tubing around his face, replacing his left eye with a small camera lens and even cast a slimy gray hue over his skin.

"Mom?"

Gabe's loud whisper shattered Emma's vision. She turned to her son. "Hmm?"

"Why are you staring at Mr. Johnson?"

Heat stung Emma's cheeks. When she glanced at Rafe to see him smiling warmly at her, all the Borg paraphernalia vanished with a *poof*. Rafe was very, very human and very, very male.

This might be harder than she thought.

* * *

Sylvia insisted Emma and Rafe leave right after supper, so they soon found themselves on the front porch, alone.

Rafe took out his keys. "Where to?"

Distracted by his assumption that he'd be the one driving, Emma said, "Max's?"

As soon as the name of the small café just off Overton Square left her lips, she wanted to stuff it back in. She hadn't been to Max's in years. Six and a half years, to be exact. She and Rafe spent a lot of time there when they'd dated, mostly because there was virtually no danger of running into anyone who knew her parents.

Dismayed by how easily she'd slipped back into old habits, she barely noticed when Rafe placed a hand at the back of her waist.

The pressure he applied eased almost immediately, however, as his breath hissed in. "We've been there before, haven't we?"

The faraway look in his eyes told her he was experiencing another memory. It was the first time she'd actually seen it happen—when she knew what it was. The fact that the memory was triggered by his hand on her back amazed her, and at the same time made chills run down her spine. "Yes."

"Several times."

"It was our favorite place to meet. It was quiet, the food was good and cheap, and we never knew anyone who came in." She looked away, embarrassed by her choice, knowing he would assume she'd selected the café for sentimental reasons.

His hand moved ever so slightly on her back, telling her she was right. She didn't expect the jolt of heat his caress sent shooting through her. Startled, she pulled away from his touch and started down the steps. "Why don't we go for a walk instead?"

He followed. "I'd like to see this place, if you don't mind."

She did mind, but didn't want to tell him the reasons why. "Do you remember how to get there?"

"No."

She gave him simple directions as he unlocked the passenger

door of his truck. He opened it, waited for her to climb onto the bench seat, then closed it. The gentlemanly gesture made memories of her own spring to mind. Rafe used to insist on opening doors and pulling out chairs for her. His consideration had always made her feel feminine, cared for.

It still did. Damn. Where was women's lib when she needed it?

She buckled her seat belt as he climbed behind the steering wheel, buckled in and started the engine.

Closed in the small space with him suddenly seemed achingly familiar, and unbearably intimate. Though she was looking out the windshield instead of at him, she was acutely aware of every move he made, every breath he took.

"Has Memphis grown much since I've been gone?" he asked as he drove down the street.

Small talk. How could she make small talk when all she wanted to do was say what needed to be said so she could escape before she did something really stupid—like throw herself into his arms. "By leaps and bounds, but mostly out east where you're staying. Cordova, Collierville, Germantown. Midtown hasn't changed very much."

"I lived downtown, didn't I? On Mud Island."

"Yes. Your apartment had a wonderful view of the river." She'd loved his apartment. Loved cooking him supper when she could make excuses not to eat at home. Loved watching the Mississippi River meander past as she stood in the circle of his arms. Loved making love by the lights of the Tennessee-Arkansas bridge streaming in his window.

She started to suggest he rent another apartment in that same complex, then remembered her decision.

Before she could change her mind, she blurted out, "If the offer still stands, I'd like to accept the job working on *Southern Yesteryears*."

He threw a sharp glance in her direction, but took so long to answer, she winced. "You've changed your mind."

"No," he said quickly. "I definitely haven't changed my mind. In fact, I've been wondering for the last hour how I was going to talk you into accepting. What made you change yours? My sparkling dinner conversation?"

"No, I...we need a new roof."

"That's right." He almost sounded disappointed. "Well, whatever the reason, I'm glad. Thank you."

"You're welcome."

As he turned onto Cooper, she breathed a sigh of mixed anxiety and relief. She'd have to live with the consequences now. She knew he'd never let her go back on her word. But at least the indecision was over.

"Have you thought any more about renting me a couple of rooms?"

Emma hesitated, still uncertain about sharing so much of her life with this man. To have him living in the house would—

"Wait a minute," she said suddenly.

He jerked his foot off the gas. "What for?"

"Sorry, I was thinking out loud. What about the carriage house? There are two large rooms, plus a bathroom, above the garage. They were used by servants when we had them. I was up there just a month ago, checking for leaks. Those rooms are in better shape than most of those in the main house. They're even furnished. They need to be thoroughly cleaned but I can do that before you—"

"I'll get a professional cleaning crew," he insisted.

"Then the carriage house is okay?" He'd still be on the premises, but not in the house. Surely she could deal with that.

"I don't see why not."

"And you'll still pay for the roof?"

He smiled. "I'll still pay for the roof. But I have one more request."

She regarded him warily. "What?"

"I wonder if your mother would cook for me. Nothing special.

Just what the family's eating. I'll help pay for groceries, of course." He lifted a rueful brow. "I can't cook worth a darn."

"Yes, I remember," she murmured.

"What?"

"Nothing." She sighed. "I'm sure you can talk my mother into cooking anything for you. She's on your side, you know."

His smile widened. "Is she?"

"I wouldn't be so flattered, if I were you. Momma defines the class of old-fashioned Southern women. Any male would suit her, as long as he's got good teeth and nice manners."

"Then I'll remember to brush my teeth and say, 'Yes, ma'am.'"

"I probably shouldn't have told you," she grumbled. "No doubt you'll use it to your advantage."

"No doubt."

Emma watched him as he concentrated on fitting his full-size truck into the small parking lot of the coffeehouse. "Rafe..."

"Hmm?"

"I want you to understand that this arrangement is strictly professional. I need a job, and you need an artist."

He glanced at her. "I need a place to stay, and you have a place to rent."

She nodded, relieved he understood. "A business arrangement. Nothing more."

His brow wrinkled in thought, he killed the engine and released his seat belt. "What about my memories? Is helping me part of this deal?"

She took her time releasing her own seat belt. "What would I need to do?"

"Let me touch you," he said quietly. "That's what seems to trigger them."

Emma swallowed hard and tried to will her pulse to keep an even beat. "What do you mean, touch?"

"Something like..." He reached across and laced his fingers through hers. "Like this."

Emma had forgotten what a sensual experience the simple act of holding hands could be. The feel of his flesh against hers made heat wrap around her heart like a cocoon. Their fingers were meshed together so completely it was hard to tell where her flesh ended and his began. She wanted to draw him closer, to feel his warmth on more than just her hand.

With an effort she drew her mind away from the contact. "Are you remembering anything?"

"We used to hold hands a lot, didn't we? I remember several times—walking into my apartment, waiting on chairs in some office, riding in my car."

She pulled in a ragged breath. "Maybe this isn't such a good idea."

"Why?" he demanded softly. "Because you like it as much as I do?"

That was exactly the reason. "Rafe, we shouldn't—"

"The hell we shouldn't." He scooted out from under the wheel and lifted her onto his lap. "I've wanted to taste you ever since you walked into that conference room."

"But I—"

"Shhh." He slowly drew a finger down her cheek, his face full of wonder. "How could I have forgotten you? How could I have forgotten this?..."

Mesmerized by his warm breath against her face and the fire in his coal-dark eyes, Emma watched his lips descend.

Chapter Five

When their lips met, memories exploded in Rafe's head like the grand finale of a July Fourth fireworks extravaganza. He kissed Emma so many times in the space of a few seconds that his head began to reel.

He held on tighter.

Then, just as rapidly as they'd come, the memories melted under the relentless heat generated by the friction of his body against hers. The past became irrelevant because suddenly nothing mattered except the woman in his arms.

The warm flesh pressed against him was real, and a hell of a lot better than any memory could ever be. His blood burned through his veins like wildfire, and the oxygen they shared scorched his lungs.

Her arms trapped between them, Emma twisted handfuls of his shirt as if trying to pull him closer.

He saved her the trouble, wrapping his arms around her slender back and deepening the kiss.

When they came up for air, she whimpered and struggled to free her arms.

Disappointment doused the highest flames, and he let her draw away.

But instead of freeing herself, she wrapped her arms around his neck. "Damn you."

His heart raced like a printing press at full speed at this sweet evidence of her desire. "What?"

"You taste the same," she said on half a sob, then pulled his lips back down to hers. She opened her mouth against his, inviting him in.

Desire roared through his body as his tongue delved into the sweet recesses of her mouth. He crushed her against him, feeling her breasts push into his chest.

They groaned in unison. Rafe dropped his hands to her hips and pressed her against the raging length of his desire. It had been so long—forever—since he'd had a woman in his arms.

Dimly, in the recesses of his mind, he recognized that his control was rapidly slipping away, but it took several minutes to remember why it mattered. Finally he realized what he was doing, and where.

He pulled away reluctantly.

Breathing hard, he buried his face in the silk of her hair and tried to bring his libido under control. Her hot breath against his neck didn't help.

Gradually oxygen began to clear his mind, and he realized she was rigid in his arms.

"I'm sorry," he breathed. "I didn't intend to let it go so—"

"Damn you."

Emma struggled to free herself, and he let her go. She immediately began fumbling to open the truck door.

He grabbed her arm. "Where are you going?"

"Let go of me."

"What's wrong?"

"What's wrong?" She turned amazed eyes on him. "You kissed me."

"And you kissed me. So? It's not like we committed treason."

Emma looked away from his burning eyes. What she'd just done *was* treason—treason against her own principles. She'd thrown herself into his arms as quickly as she had when she was nineteen, and she'd loved being there twice as much.

Panicked by the realization that she was just as attracted to Rafe as she'd ever been, she jerked her arm away. Shoving the truck door open, she fled toward the relative safety of the café.

She heard his door slam and a Spanish expletive before the restaurant door shut out the sound. She stood just inside, breathing deeply, trying to recover her composure—her distance—before he caught up.

"Emma? Emma Grey, is that you?"

Another voice from the past drew her attention to the owner of the café, who moved around the counter toward her.

A cross between a redneck and a hippie, he looked exactly the same as the last time she'd seen him, with the exception of a few more gray hairs framing his temple and a few extra pounds.

"Hello, Max." Her soft smile stiffened when she heard the door open behind her.

"Well, hot damn, it is you. I haven't seen you in a coon's age. And there's— Hell's bells, Rafe. You look like you been put through the coffee grinder. What happened?"

Rafe came up behind her. Placing a hand on her back, he extended his other to meet Max's. "An assignment gone bad. Nice to see you again."

Emma wondered if he remembered Max or was faking it.

His next words told her. "You still make the best hamburgers in the continental United States?"

Suddenly she realized why he'd put his hand on her back—so he could remember the café and its owner. Already raw from their wrangling in the truck, she felt used, and pulled away from his touch.

Max grinned and rubbed the grizzled chin lost in the folds of his neck. "Sure do. Y'all want the old usual?"

"Actually, we just ate," Rafe told him. "We'll take a rain

check on the burgers. How about a couple of your fried pies and some coffee?''

"Coming up."

"Just coffee for me," Emma said. "Decaf."

Max nodded. "Sure thing. Your booth is over there waiting on you. I'll be right out with the eats."

Emma turned to Rafe and lifted a brow, challenging him to lead them to "their" booth.

He led the way unerringly, then waited until she'd seated herself before sliding onto the seat opposite her.

She stalled for time. "So you remembered."

He nodded, peering around with interest. "It hasn't changed, has it? This bench is still as hard as ever."

In the face of his obvious wonder, it was hard to stay mad at him for using her to regain his memories. She had much more important things to focus her anger on. But she didn't want to get into that until Max had come and gone.

Fortunately, he came right out.

"Where've you two been?" he asked as he placed the coffee and pie on the table. "I haven't seen y'all in—must be six or seven years."

"We moved out of town," Rafe told him.

"You couldn't come tell old Max goodbye?"

Rafe shrugged. "Sorry. I guess we got caught up in all the details. I got a job at the *Denver Post* and had to leave on assignment."

Max nodded. "You two ever get married? I don't see no wedding rings."

Rafe met Emma's eyes across the table. "It's a long story. We'll fill you in another time, all right?"

"Sure thing. Nice to see you again." Taking the hint, Max moved away to check on his other customers.

Rafe held onto Emma's gaze. "You going to tell me why you sprinted from the car like an Olympic runner?"

"You know why. We'd just agreed to keep our relationship strictly business, then you go and—" Heat crept up her neck.

"You can't even say it, can you? I kissed you."

"Exactly."

Rafe glared at her. He sure as hell didn't feel like apologizing. She was his wife, damn it, and she'd enjoyed their kiss every bit as much as he had. Until her brain got in the way.

He dropped his gaze to his coffee. But he'd promised himself he'd keep his libido under control. He needed to be her friend, not her lover. The relationship he wanted with her was more important than momentary physical gratification.

Besides, how far would he have taken it? If she'd got a glimpse of what was beneath his shirt, she'd have shot out of his truck for entirely different reasons.

"Maybe us working together isn't such a good idea," she said.

His head came up. "Oh, no, you don't. You accepted the job, and I'm keeping you to your promise."

"Why should I keep my promise when you don't keep yours?"

"What promise?"

"To keep our relationship all business."

"I never actually agreed to that, if you'll recall."

Her eyes narrowed. "If you think that just because some piece of paper says we're married you have an express train to my bedroom, you're in for a rude awakening. I can't afford a lawyer right now, but as soon as I can, I'll—"

"There's no point in discussing it now." He didn't want her to utter the word *divorce*. Couldn't stand the thought of losing this phenomenal connection to her, to his newly discovered family. "Look, I'm sorry. I got carried away. I didn't even mean to kiss you, much less let it go so far. I won't let it happen again. I swear."

Her face was filled with uncertainty. "How can I trust you after...what happened?"

"Can you trust yourself?" he asked bluntly. "You participated in that kiss just as much as I did."

She looked away. "I know. I..."

He reached across the table for her hand. "What's so wrong with a little kiss?"

She yanked her hand out of reach. "That was not a *little* kiss. If we'd been in a more private place, who knows what would've happened?"

"Not what you're thinking." He couldn't keep the bitterness from his voice. The thought of her reaction to his scarred, mangled body made something inside him freeze. "I'm not ready to hop in bed with anyone right now, believe me."

"Well, I sure couldn't tell that from the way you kissed me."

He shrugged. "Like I said, I got a little carried away. I'm sorry."

His apology must've finally penetrated, because she visibly calmed. After a moment spent looking anywhere but at him, she said, "I didn't mean to insult you. I just can't deal with another man in my life right now. I can barely keep my own head above water—plus I'm responsible for Momma, Gabe and that money pit we call a house. I don't have the time or the energy to take on anything or anyone else."

"I can help with—"

"No!" Obviously realizing she'd spoken a bit too vehemently, she brought her voice down. "I can take care of myself and my family. I'll help you with your magazine and maybe, sometimes, help you with your memories. But only if I'm the one who touches you, not the other way around. I don't want a repeat of what just happened in your truck."

Rafe felt as if he'd just been slapped. *Her*self. *Her* family. She couldn't have made it clearer—she had no use for him. She didn't need him or anything he had to offer, except the damn job. Hurt, and angry because of it, he sat back in the booth. "The family you're so capable of taking care of is my family, too."

Her gaze dropped to his untouched pie. "That's just a technicality. As soon as I can afford it, I'll hire a lawyer and—"

"Technicality, hell. Gabe is my son. I have an obligation, and a right, to take care of him and to have him as a part of my life."

Her fists struck the table. "I knew you'd do this. I knew you'd waltz in here and try to worm your way back into my life, so you can take over everything like you always did."

"What the hell do you expect me to do? Walk away? Act like I don't have a wife and son? Tell me, Emma, is that what the man you fell in love with would've done?"

She deflated like a balloon with a fast leak. "That man doesn't exist anymore. Neither does the girl who fell in love with him. You don't even remember her."

She was right. He wasn't the same man he'd been. Hell, he couldn't even remember who that man was. And she must've changed, as well. But knowing that didn't stop him from wanting to reach across the table and touch her. From wanting to drag her into his arms and kiss her misgivings away. But he couldn't. Even though he was her husband, he didn't have the right. He might never have the right.

"Please, Rafe..."

He shook off the depressing thoughts and leaned forward. He couldn't let the tears glistening in her green eyes dissuade him from his purpose. "I don't care what you say. As Gabe's father, I have certain rights."

She sucked in a horrified breath. "You're not going to try and take him away from me?"

"No, of course not." He ran a hand back through his hair. "I want to get to know my son, Emma. I want him to know me. Don't you think I have that right?"

"You're going to be living at the house. What more do you want?"

"I want to hear him call me Dad," he said softly.

"He...he thinks Jerry's his father."

Rafe's face tightened. "He's not."

"I know, but...Please. Give me time to tell Gabe in my own way."

He hesitated. "How much time?"

"I don't know. Until we figure out what we're going to do."

"About what?"

"About this...mess we're in."

His eyes narrowed. "Mess? That's what I am to you?"

She lifted her chin. "You've only been risen from the dead for three days. After six and a half years thinking I was your widow, I need some time to get my thoughts straight on what I should do."

Rafe sat back and studied her solemn face. He didn't want to give her another minute. He wanted his family, and he wanted it now. After all this time not knowing who the hell he was, didn't he deserve it?

But if he pushed the issue now, she was sure to dig in her heels. Maybe time wasn't such a bad idea. He'd be spending the next few months in her back pocket. They'd be working together every day. Time would let her get to know him, would let her see she didn't have anything to fear from him. Meanwhile, he'd also be with Gabe. He could get to know his son, even if Gabe didn't know he was his father.

"All right," he said quietly.

A brief flash of surprise crossed her face, then she relaxed in obvious relief. "Thank you."

He nodded, then with nothing better to do, took a sip of coffee. It was cold. "So."

She studied his face warily, then repeated, "So?"

"Do you have someone to fix the roof, or should I find someone?"

She relaxed even more as she realized their intimate discussion was over—for now. "We got estimates three months ago. I know who to call."

"Fine. Call them tomorrow."

"I will."

"I'd like to move into the carriage house this weekend, if I could. Then I won't have to pay for another week at the motel. Even though it's an extended-stay facility, it's still expensive."

"All right. I'll get up there after work tomorrow and start cleaning—"

"No, you won't. I told you I'll hire a professional company. I'll make a few calls tomorrow. I can probably get someone there Friday."

She shrugged. "Whatever."

"About computer equipment...I don't know what to get. Can you research that and order whatever you need?"

Her eyes lit up. "What's the budget?"

"Will ten thousand dollars be enough?"

"Ten thousand? I can get something that will do for half that."

He shook his head. "From what I hear, it's better to get the best up front. So buy what you need."

She smiled, her eyes beginning to glow. "This could be fun."

The next afternoon, Emma turned into the driveway and pulled along the narrow drive to the carriage house in the back. The garage door was open, as usual, but before she could pull in, a flash of movement in the backyard made her step on the brake.

Rafe was playing catch with Gabe. Both were dressed in jeans, shirts and baseball caps. The only difference was Rafe had on a long-sleeved shirt.

They looked so much alike.

Emma groaned. She was hoping she'd have a day or two before seeing Rafe again. How was she supposed to deal with this man when he didn't give her time to recover from all the feelings he aroused in her?

She closed her eyes against the memory of his lips touching hers the night before. Of his warm body—broader and harder than she remembered—under her all-too-sensitive hands. Of his very male scent smoking her senses, driving out her will to—

A rap on the window made her gasp, snapping her out of her daydream. Her eyes flew open to see the star of her dreams leaning down next to the car.

"You okay?" he asked.

She lowered the window. "What are you doing here?"

He lifted a dark brow at her accusing tone. "I found a cleaning crew that could come this afternoon. They finished half an hour ago."

She sighed. "I suppose my mother invited you to stay for supper."

"Meals were part of the agreement, remember?"

"*After* you moved in."

He reached into his pocket, then dangled a key in the window. "I'm officially your tenant."

Her hands clenched the steering wheel. "You've already moved in?"

"Not quite yet. I'm having some new furniture delivered tomorrow. A decent bed and a new desk. I won't check out of the motel until Saturday. Gabe talked me into taking him and Randy swimming in the pool there on Saturday, if it's all right with—"

"No," Emma said quickly.

Rafe's first instinct was relief. He'd been trying all afternoon to talk Gabe into something other than swimming, knowing how much of his body was exposed in swimming trunks. Though he'd been swimming to keep his heart strong, it was in his parents' pool in their secluded backyard. He'd swum several times since he'd been in Memphis, but only when the motel pool was deserted.

Then he realized what Emma was doing. She was trying to keep his son away from him. Suddenly he was determined to take his son to the pool. He'd wear a wet suit if he had to. "They're real excited about it. Gabe said he doesn't get to go swimming much so I—"

"You shouldn't have promised him." Her chin lifted. "He can't go."

"Why?" he asked bluntly. "Afraid I'm going to let my son drown?"

"No, I..."

Emma was afraid of just the opposite—that Rafe would drown Gabe with attention, and that Gabe would love it, would love him.

Her son was hungry for a man's attention. That's why she'd enrolled him in T-ball, thinking he could get all that male bonding stuff from his teammates and coach. Rafe was back in their lives now and could give her son what he so desperately needed—but for how long?

He was here because he wanted his memories. But she was worried what would happen if he got them. She didn't know the man who'd barged into their lives. He seemed to want his son, but he hadn't been around when Gabe was growing up. How was he going to react when the going got rough? When the newness wore off and Gabe got sick and cranky? Or misbehaved in a child's natural striving for independence?

The Rafe she knew she'd have trusted not to bail out on her. But not this one. Not yet.

And if he left after winning Gabe's love and trust, what would happen to her son?

Better to keep father and son apart as much as possible, and to be around when she couldn't avoid their being together. That way, Gabe's innocent, trusting heart would be safe. Like hers was going to be.

She placed her hand on the window button. "I'm wasting gas."

Rafe leaned closer, his face hard. "Emma, if you don't give me access to my son, I'll have to—"

"Rafe?" Gabe called. "You coming back?"

Rafe straightened and half turned to reply. "Just a minute."

Emma seized the opportunity to end the conversation and stepped on the accelerator. She took her time gathering her things, and by the time she lowered the garage door, Rafe was again pitching to Gabe.

She'd leave them alone for now. They were so boisterous, they couldn't be bonding.

She breathed a sigh, ragged with both relief and worry. This was what life was going to be like in the foreseeable future. Constantly on guard to protect herself and her son.

Just the thought made her so tired her shoulders slumped as she walked into the house.

Rafe pulled off his baseball cap, then pushed open the back door. He turned to see his son slowly making his way toward the house, tossing the ball in the air and catching it. "Get a move on, Gabe. Your grandmother called us in five minutes ago."

"I'm coming," the boy grumbled. He finally pulled off his glove and climbed the back stairs, then threw the ball and glove on the nearest chair.

"Is that where your equipment is stored?" Rafe asked.

"Awww, jeeeez." After giving him a look that said *Not you, too,* Gabe picked up his things and placed them in the old wicker chest that held his outside toys.

"If you don't take care of your baseball, it won't last very long." Rafe removed his son's cap as the boy entered the house. "Go get washed up, okay?"

"Okay." Acting as if he was going to his execution, Gabe walked down the hall to the bathroom.

Rafe couldn't help smiling as he watched until the door closed. Gabe was full of energy as long as he was playing, but quickly ran out when it came to chores or something distasteful like washing some part of his body.

Shaking his head, Rafe followed the smell of corn bread into the kitchen.

"Sure smells good," he told Sylvia.

She smiled at him. "Thanks for looking after Gabe for a while.

It can be mighty tough keeping an eye on him while I'm cooking. He's quite a handful.''

Rafe placed their caps on the counter, then leaned against it. ''You can say that again. I was just wondering if I was that rambunctious when I was his age.''

''Probably.''

''What can I do to help?'' he asked her.

She waved away his offer. ''I've got it under control.''

He'd already discovered that Sylvia had definite views about ''men's work'' and ''women's work.'' But he had to ask. His own mother expected her sons to wash dishes right along with her daughter and also expected her daughter to help mow the lawn.

Rafe wasn't exactly thrilled that his son was being raised in such a chauvinistic way, but if he asserted his parental authority, Emma would accuse him of trying to run her life.

''Were you always the cook around here?'' he asked. ''Living in a house like this, I would think you'd have had servants.''

''Bless me, yes. I had a cook right up until the day Cecil's will was read. A maid, too, though neither of them lived in.'' She sighed. ''I had to let them go when we found out how much money we didn't have.''

''What happened, if you don't mind me asking? Your husband was the president of Memphis Savings and Loan, wasn't he?''

She nodded. ''I guess he spent all our money maintaining our standing in the community. Social life was very important to Cecil. More important than providing for his family, I guess.''

''I'm sorry.''

She shrugged. ''We get along. Besides, I always liked to cook. And dig in the dirt. When I was a little girl, I'd either be in here stirring peas or outside planting marigolds.''

''So you're the one who keeps the yard so nice.''

''I'd put in a vegetable garden if there was a corner of the yard that got enough sun. Nothing like okra fresh off the stalk.''

"Well, you're good at gardening, but I especially like your cooking." He snitched a piece of the corn bread she'd just cut.

Instead of chastising him like his own mother would've, she beamed. "Thank you, son. Here, try it with some honey."

There were definite pluses to the old Southern viewpoint, he thought as he drizzled honey on the hot corn bread.

"I saw you talking to Emma," Sylvia said.

He hesitated. Though he felt disloyal discussing their problems with Emma's mother, he needed an ally. Since Emma knew about their past and he didn't, he needed all the help he could get.

"She won't let me take Gabe and Randy swimming on Saturday."

Sylvia shook her head. "That girl."

"What's wrong, Sylvia? Why doesn't she trust me enough to take my own son to a pool?"

She glanced at him, her lips pressed together. Emma said Sylvia was on his side. He was about to find out how much. Would she confide in him?

Finally Sylvia nodded, as if making a decision. She stepped over to the door and glanced down the hall, then turned back to him. "Emma wouldn't let Billy Graham take Gabe to Sunday School. She just doesn't trust people anymore—especially men."

"Why? Because I left her? I couldn't help it."

Sylvia shrugged as she went back to the stove. "You're part of it, but not all. She's had some rough times in the past six and a half years, mostly with Jerry and Cecil. It hasn't been easy for any of us, but she's the one that had the brunt of their...behavior. And she's had to shoulder the burden ever since."

"What happened with...Jerry, was it? Why did she marry him?"

Sylvia took the lid off a pot of stew and stirred it. "Cecil made her. He couldn't stand the thought of everyone knowing his grandchild was sired by a...by you. Emma held out until they officially called off the search for you. Then she sort of gave up. I think she just wanted to get away from her father."

Needing to know what he was up against, Rafe couldn't help pressing for information. "How long was she married?"

"Almost two years. Gabe was about eighteen months old when she left Jerry."

"She didn't love him, did she?"

"No. They'd known each other since they were little, but they were never in love."

Relief flowed through him like a narcotic. He hadn't realized until that moment how important Emma's feelings for Jerry were to him. "Why did she leave him?"

Sylvia set the large spoon on a small plate. "She never said for sure, but she keeps talking about how men want to control women. She says they're like the Borg, whoever they are."

"On *Star Trek*," he told her, half his mind on the implications of Sylvia's revelations. "They're these creatures who—"

He broke off at the sound of a door opening.

Two pairs of footsteps came down the hall, one running, one walking.

Gabe entered first. "Is supper ready?"

"Just about," his grandmother told him.

The boy rubbed his stomach. "I love stew. Do you like stew, Rafe?"

Rafe grabbed his son and threw him in the air. "I sure do."

Gabe squealed with delight.

As Rafe set him back on the floor, Emma entered. Her gaze immediately clashed with his. He held onto it, trying to see past the green shutters to the wounded woman hidden inside. He wished he could've been there for her, to relieve her of the burdens she'd taken on her slender shoulders.

But she wouldn't let him help with anything. Wouldn't even tell him she needed help. She'd planted her mistrust so deep, lived with it so long, she probably wasn't even aware it was a problem.

Could he overcome such an obstacle?

He had to, or risk losing the family he'd so recently found. He had to find some way to teach her how to trust again. At least to trust him. He had to show her that he didn't want control of her life, just control of his own. She was the only one who could help him get it back.

Emma tore her gaze away and reached into a cabinet for plates. Rafe opened the drawer behind him that held the silverware.

How did one go about teaching someone else to trust?

He supposed by being trustworthy. That meant he couldn't let her avoid him. In order for her to learn to trust him, she had to be around him. And she had to let him be around his son.

So the first thing he had to do was confront her about this weekend. He could hide most of his damaged body if he wore a T-shirt for "protection against the sun" and got into the pool before they arrived so his legs were obscured by the water.

As they set the table, he debated on how to bring the subject up when Gabe saved him the trouble.

As he placed the napkins at each place, Gabe looked at his mother, his dark eyes dancing. "Mom, Rafe's gonna take Randy and me to his pool on Saturday."

Emma threw Rafe a nasty look. "He is, is he?"

"Yeah. He said there's a slide and everything! Randy called his mom today, and she said it's okay with her if it's okay with you."

"Sure. Let me be the bad guy," she murmured.

"What's that?" Sylvia asked as she came in with the plate of corn bread.

"Nothing." Emma placed the last plate on the table. "I'm sorry, Gabe. Y'all won't be able to go."

"Mom!" Gabe cried. "Why?"

"Aw, honey," Sylvia said. "It's all the boys could talk about all day."

"I'm sure." Emma turned the plate so the design faced her. "I have too much work to do. I found a computer system at lunch today. I was hoping Rafe could pick it up tomorrow, so I can spend Saturday installing software."

Rafe shook his head. "I can't go tomorrow. I've got a meeting in the morning with a possible printer, and furniture coming tomorrow afternoon."

She looked so dismayed, he felt like he'd won the argument by cheating. He wanted to win it by making her trust him. Then it occurred to him that he could start showing her how to trust him by trusting her.

He reached into his wallet and took out a credit card. "Here. You go pick it up."

She looked at his card as if she'd never seen one before. "I can't use your card."

"Sure you can." His mouth twisted. "Just sign it Mrs. Rafe Johnson."

Her eyes widened, and she threw a warning glance toward her son, who watched them with curious eyes.

Seeing he was unmoved, she lifted her chin. "That's not my name."

He held the card steady. "No?"

She frowned at him. "Computer boxes are huge. I can't fit them all in my car."

"If you pay for it, so it's ready to load, I can swing by and pick it up."

"Then why can't you pay—"

"I won't have time. If you go at lunch and pick everything out and pay for it, they'll have it ready to go."

Emma finally took the card. "I can't believe you're just handing over your card. It's the one without a limit, isn't it? I could buy anything."

"I trust you," he said simply.

She studied his face, as if trying to decide what planet he'd come from.

He cleared his throat. "Now, back to our discussion..."

She rolled her eyes. "I told you, I don't have time to go swimming. It takes most of a day to set up a system like this. If I don't do it this weekend, I'll have to wait a whole week, which will delay me starting on the magazine.''

"You don't need to go to the pool with us," Rafe pointed out. If he couldn't be with her, at least he could spend time with Gabe.

"Yes, I do."

"Why?"

"Motel pools rarely have lifeguards. What if something happened?"

"I'll be there."

"But you're—" she pressed her lips together, then went ahead and said it ''—not in the best physical condition.''

His eyes narrowed. He'd be damned if he'd let her use his bum leg to keep him from spending time with his son. If she was going to win this argument, she was going to have to come right out and say she didn't trust him—in front of their son. "I move just fine in the water. In fact, that's how I've been keeping in shape. That and lifting weights. My parents have a pool, and I swam every day."

"But—"

"Are you crazy, Mom?" Gabe cried. "Rafe can swim. He can do anything."

Emma frowned at her son. "Rafe isn't some superhero, Gabe. I just—"

"No, but even President Roosevelt, who was crippled with polio, could swim," he said.

"Gracious me, Emma." Sylvia crossed her arms over her stomach. "You can take off a couple hours on Saturday to go swimming with these boys. Rafe isn't such a slave driver as that."

"Thank you, Sylvia." He smiled at his collaborator, then turned back to Emma. "I didn't expect the system to be up and running for another week, anyway. We have plenty of time."

"But the sooner we get started, the sooner you'll have something to show potential advertisers."

"My schedule will allow a few hours for a swim on Saturday. If you don't finish then, can't you do the rest on Sunday?"

Cornered, Emma glared at him. Was she so reluctant to trust him that she'd shatter her son's expectations?

"Please!" Gabe cried. "I'll go to bed on time tonight."

Emma glanced at her son's anxious face, then closed her eyes and took a deep breath. Finally, through clenched teeth, she said, "Fine."

Rafe actually felt proud of her for giving in. Maybe teaching her to trust him wouldn't take as long as he'd thought. "You're coming, too, aren't you?"

"You can bet your Speedo."

He smiled. "If I have to wear a Speedo, you have to wear a bikini."

Gabe giggled.

Emma's eyes narrowed. "My bathing suit is thick and black and comes to my knees."

He chuckled. "Oh, well. I can dream, can't I?"

Chapter Six

Rafe leaned back in the rolling chair he'd just assembled to enjoy the view.

Emma's derriere was at eye level, just an arm's reach away. Her jeans were stretched tight as she bent around the computer to plug in the wires attaching the scanner. Round and luscious, the curves dared him to touch. And, God help him, he could barely restrain his hands from taking the dare.

A gentleman would discreetly avert his eyes, but at the moment he didn't feel very gentlemanly. He wanted to pull her onto his lap where his own jeans were getting tighter by the second and cover her mouth with his. He wanted to drag her T-shirt over her head and fill his hands with—

"How's it feel?"

"Damn, I wish I knew," he whispered.

She straightened and twisted to look at him. "What?"

His daydream shattered, he blinked. "What?"

Her brow furrowed. "The chair. How does it feel?"

"Oh." He glanced down at the blue armrests. "Great. Want to try it?"

She shook her head. "I'll be in it enough when I'm installing software."

"What can I do to help you finish?"

She sent him a dubious glance. "Can you get under the desk and plug everything into the surge protector? I just let all the plugs dangle back there."

His mouth twisted wryly. "I think I can manage."

"I'm sorry. I don't know what you can or can't do."

His smile faded. She really did think he was crippled. This was exactly what he'd been afraid of. She wasn't focusing on him as a man, she was focusing on his injuries. "I can do just about everything you can. Maybe not as well or as quickly, but I get along. Except run. I can't run."

"You used to run every day to keep in shape."

"That's what I understand." He shrugged. "Now I swim and lift weights."

She nodded.

He dropped to his knees and crawled under the new computer table to plug in the cords. "There sure are a lot of wires back here."

"I know," she said from behind him. "That's one drawback with computers. Everything has to have its own separate plug, and it gets to be a real mess."

He fitted all the plugs he could find into the surge protector. "There's five, right?"

"Hmm?" she murmured absently.

He backed up and twisted enough to see her. She was staring at his rear end. So she *was* thinking of him as a man. A smile of deep male satisfaction broke across his face. "Either kick it or grab it. The suspense is killing me."

Her wide eyes rose to his. "What?"

"You were examining my butt like you were thinking about buying it. Go ahead." He flexed his gluteus maximus. "You can touch the merchandise."

Crimson crept up her neck to stain her cheeks, and her eyes

narrowed. She picked up a large piece of foam that had protected the monitor and broke it across his butt. "Here's my touch."

He emitted an exaggerated moan of pleasure. "More."

She laughed and quirked her brow. "Into kinky sex now, are you?"

He leaned back on his heels. "Whatever clicks your mouse."

"Oh, be quiet." Emma threw the broken piece of Styrofoam at him, then rose. His sexy, daring smile was so provocative, so familiar, she could barely keep herself from falling to her knees and seeing how many times she could wrap herself around him.

"There were five plugs, right?" he asked again.

She had to stop and count. Monitor, CPU, printer, scanner and backup drive. "Five. Right."

"Then it's ready to go."

She inserted the tools disk into the external backup drive, then turned all the peripherals on. After giving them a few seconds to warm up, she pressed the power key on the keyboard. A deep-throated chord chimed from the tower as the unit began to hum.

She turned to Rafe with a smile. "It's alive."

He rose to his knees, peering at the computer as if it were a being from a distant galaxy. "Is that good?"

She chuckled. "It means we did everything right. So far."

"You mean *you* did everything right. I just watched. You seemed to know what you were doing."

"I do," she said with confidence.

"I'm glad someone does."

As he slowly lifted himself to his feet, he paused. "Who's that?"

Emma heard the distinct sound of someone climbing the stairs to Rafe's apartment. "Too heavy to be Gabe or Momma. Are you expecting any more deliveries?"

"Not today. At least I know no one can sneak up on me." He walked into the small entryway and opened the wooden door. "Jay Patten. How the hell did you find me so fast? I just moved in today."

Surprise made Emma blink. Who was this? She thought Rafe didn't remember anyone in Memphis. Though she leaned to the side, she could hear puffing but couldn't see Rafe's friend.

"I've still got a few investigative skills left from my reporter days," said a deep voice with a thick Southern accent.

"Come on in." Rafe led the man into the room. "Emma, this is Jay Patten. We worked together years ago at the *Commercial Appeal*. Jay, this is Emma, the competent half of this operation."

Jay had a round face—which at the moment was red—a round body and round dark eyes. He and Rafe looked like "before and after" pictures in some fitness ad. "Ah, she must be your computer expert."

Rafe met her eyes across the room. "Emma's the best graphic artist in Memphis. She's setting up the computer system."

"Ah. Better her than us, huh, old buddy?"

Emma shook her head, trying to keep her insides from melting at the warmth of Rafe's confident praise. She hoped she could live up to his expectations. "I don't understand how two grown men could live in this day and age and not know how to plug in a computer. Don't you use one at the newspaper?"

"Sure do," Jay told her. "But we have a whole department of people to handle all that technical stuff. To me it's just a glorified typewriter."

"Let's sit down." Rafe cleared the old couch of the stuff Emma had thrown on it as she dug into the boxes.

She stepped over to rescue the manuals. "I can come back later if you—"

"You won't bother us," Rafe said. "Besides, you need to finish by four if you can, so we can take Gabe."

With a heavy sigh of relief, Jay settled on one end of the couch. "Who's Gabe?"

Rafe sent her another I'd-sure-as-hell-like-to-tell-him look, then said, "He's Emma's son. We're taking him swimming at the motel. I haven't checked out yet."

Pulling her attention away from the two men, Emma dug

through the debris for the software boxes. She couldn't help but notice that Rafe never lied about his relationship to her and Gabe. He told just enough of the truth to satisfy whoever he was talking to.

As she tore the plastic wrap off the screen saver, she remembered how honest he'd always been. He'd told her that as a reporter searching for the truth from his sources, how could he expect any less of himself? It was one trait she'd always admired, and it bothered her to know he still had it. Bothered her because she didn't want to admire him any more than she already did.

Installing software was a boring task, consisting mostly of clicking a few times, then waiting while the computer did all the work. So for the next several hours, Emma had nothing to do but listen to the two men as they talked, mostly about Rafe's ordeal. She learned a lot of the more gruesome details he'd left out of the version he'd told her—about the condition of the village that had captured him, of the many operations it took to heal his broken body, of the years of painful rehabilitation. He talked about it so matter-of-factly, as if it had happened to someone else.

But it hadn't. Here she thought she'd had a hard time during the past six years. What she'd been through was nothing compared to what had happened to Rafe.

His stories brought home her conviction that he wasn't the man she'd loved so long ago. No one could live through what Rafe had without being fundamentally changed.

Though she'd known it all along—indeed, had counted on that fact to keep her distance from Rafe—she suddenly felt depressed.

Returning her attention to their conversation, she realized with relief it had turned to what was going on at Memphis's only daily newspaper.

Jay spent a few minutes naming the people still at the *Commercial Appeal* who'd been there when Rafe was. There weren't many. Emma knew from her experience with Rafe that reporters tended to move around a lot. Rafe had worked at four newspapers before he'd come to Memphis.

He lifted a hand helplessly at Jay. "I don't remember a single one of those people."

"You might when you see them." Jay cleared his throat. "Ham Goodman certainly remembers you."

"You said he's the international news editor, right?"

Jay nodded. "We had a long talk about you yesterday. He's in dire need of a good multilingual reporter with investigative skills. He wants you to come down and talk to him. What do you say?"

Rafe shook his head. "I can't."

"You haven't lost your writing skills," Jay pointed out. "I've read several articles you've written for these history magazines."

"There's a lot more to investigative reporting than writing," Rafe said quietly. "Besides, I can't abandon *Southern Yesteryears* before I've even gotten her off the ground."

Emma released the breath she didn't know she'd been holding. She tried to tell herself the relief she felt was due to concern over losing this job. Tried to tell herself it wasn't because she remembered all the times Rafe had traveled while he'd been a reporter—and the time he didn't come back.

"Well, we won't give up easily," Jay said. "I know you don't remember Ham, but he's one stubborn son of a—" He cut himself off with an apologetic glance at Emma.

Rafe shook his head again. "Sorry. Right now I want to concentrate on my magazine."

"Think about it." Jay clambered to his feet. "Well, I'd better get going. Great talking to you again. Nice to meet you, ma'am."

"Thank you, Jay. Same here."

Rafe followed him to the door, exchanging parting comments.

When he stepped back into the office, she couldn't help asking, "You loved being an investigative reporter. Why didn't you go back to it?"

He stopped and searched her face. "At first it was because I'd have to deal with people. Now..." He lifted a shoulder. "Investigative reporting requires an excellent memory—both short-term and long-term. Something I don't have."

She let her gaze be drawn to the monitor as the computer dinged. But her eyes didn't focus on the screen.

Rafe recalled more of his past every time he touched her. What would happen if he got all his memories? Would he return to reporting?

The thought of him leaving again on the kind of dangerous assignment that nearly killed him made Emma's blood turn to ice.

What was there to keep him from it?

Southern Yesteryears. And Gabe. And her.

No, not her. She couldn't think like that.

Surely his magazine and his son were enough to keep Rafe happy. Keep him here. Keep him alive.

Besides, he might never have all his memories. The things he'd remembered all seemed to deal with his time with her, not his time with the newspaper or with his life before her. Since recalling his past hinged on touching her, and the things he remembered were only about her, the chances were excellent he'd never get them all.

Relieved, Emma reached for the mouse, but her hand froze above it as her own words penetrated.

Keep Rafe happy. Keep him here.

When had it become so important for Rafe to remain in their lives?

"C'mon, Randy. It's fun! Honest."

Emma pushed up the sunglasses slipping down her nose and peered over the top of her book. Rafe and Gabe stood in the shallow end of the pool, trying to coax a wary Randy down the slide.

Randy didn't say anything, just stared down eight feet of curved blue plastic.

"I'll catch you like I caught Gabe," Rafe told the boy.

Randy just stared.

"Do you want to climb down?" Rafe asked.

The boy shook his head.

"Do you want Gabe to slide down with you?"

"Yeah!" Gabe cried. "That'd be fun!"

Randy blinked. He regarded his friend for a minute, then gave a quick nod.

"All right!" Gabe hurriedly splashed up the steps at the end of the pool and trotted around to the slide, pulling up the trunks that threatened to slip off his thin body.

Rafe positioned himself at the end of the slide as Gabe climbed up behind Randy.

"Geronimo!" Gabe shouted and pushed off.

Two seconds later the boys hit the water. Rafe caught one in each arm. He let Gabe go under, but he caught Randy before his face got wet.

Randy started laughing. "That was fun."

Gabe splashed his friend. "Told ya!"

Randy splashed back, then glanced up at Rafe. "Can I do it again? By myself this time?"

"As many times as you want," Rafe assured him.

The boys swam toward the steps. Emma glanced at her watch, amazed to find it had taken almost twenty minutes for Rafe to talk Randy down. When had Rafe become so patient? The Rafe she'd known would've forced the issue within five minutes.

He turned to look at her then, and her eyes hit the jagged scar slashing across his right cheek. Suddenly she knew where he'd learned patience—lying in a hospital bed, unable to move. He'd told Jay his last operation had been just a year ago, when they'd tried one last time to repair the tendons in his leg. All told, he'd had six operations in the six years since he'd been found. He had so many pins in his arms and legs from having them rebroken and reset, he set off the metal detector at the airport every time he flew.

Tears burned her eyes like they had that morning when she'd heard him tell Jay, and she dropped her gaze to the book. He'd suffered so much, physically and mentally. Yet he seemed even stronger than he was years ago, despite his handicaps.

Damn the man. Why couldn't he be bitter like most people would be? Maybe then she wouldn't feel sorry for him, wouldn't want to wrap him in her arms and make his pain go away.

Emma slipped down a little on the chaise, trying to forget everything but the heroine's peril in her bestseller.

Half an hour later Gabe cried, "Mom! Look at me!"

With a smile Emma glanced up to watch her son slip down the slide for the hundredth time.

Rafe caught Gabe almost as soon as the boy hit the water. Gabe scrambled up to stand on Rafe's shoulders, holding onto his hands, then he fell backward, hitting the water with a satisfying splash.

Water hit the end of her lounge chair, but it felt good on her feet.

Gabe bobbed to the surface, laughing. He swam over and grabbed the side of the pool at her feet. "Why don't you try it? It's fun!"

"I think the slide's just for kids, baby."

"Mom," Gabe cried plaintively. "I told you, I'm not a baby."

"You're my baby."

He rolled his eyes and hauled himself from the water. "Mom!"

"Sorry. I keep forgetting you're almost a man."

Gabe's skinny chest puffed with pride. "I play baseball."

Emma didn't have to hide her smile since Gabe ran around to climb back up the slide just as Randy slid down. T-ball was only the first step in learning baseball. Still, it wouldn't be long before he'd be in Little League, then high school, then college. He'd be a man before she knew it.

"You can call *me* baby."

She glanced over to see Rafe grinning at her from the side of the pool. His chin rested on strong forearms marred with several scars she hadn't seen. One—obviously a burn scar—reached from his left hand to his elbow. He wore a T-shirt, he said to protect the scar tissue on his body from the sun. Did that mean he had worse scars?

She shuddered at the thought.

Rafe's sexy smile faded. He pulled his arms back into the water.

Though she didn't know why, she knew she'd hurt him. To distract him, she lifted a brow. "I thought I was calling you boss."

He took the bait, though the smile he gave her held more sadness than mirth. "Well, your boss thinks you should come swimming."

Randy popped up beside him. "Yeah, Miz Lockwood, come in. It feels great!"

The water did look wonderful, especially since she was slowly simmering in the hot, humid air. Sweat slid down her back and pooled between her breasts.

"Yeah, Mom." Gabe chimed in as he swam over after sliding.

"Yeah, *Miz Lockwood*." Rafe emphasized her name, not so subtly reminding her it wasn't her name at all. "We want to see the bathing suit that comes to your knees."

Emma felt like sticking her tongue out at him, but it was more than reaction to his sarcasm. She knew she was being silly, but she didn't want to take her clothes off in front of him. She didn't have the same figure she'd had six years ago. She'd had a baby. Her breasts were fuller and her hips wider.

Which was exactly why she should go in. Let him see that she wasn't the girl he remembered. Maybe then he'd lay off the comments that kept reminding her of their past relationship. Maybe he'd stop looking at her as if he wanted to start nibbling at her toes and work his way up.

"Okay, already. I'll come in."

"All right, Mom!"

She stood and pulled her T-shirt over her head. Kicking off her thongs, she turned to see three pairs of male eyes watching her. She placed her hands on her hips. ''Y'all stop staring at me and go swim.''

''Come on, guys,'' Rafe said. ''I'll race you to the other side.''

Emma quickly pushed off her shorts and turned, planning to dive into the water before the race was finished. Her first step faltered as Rafe stopped in the middle of the pool and glanced back to see how the boys were doing. She stopped altogether when his gaze caught on her.

The boys swam noisily by him, but as far as she could tell he never noticed. He stared at her as if he'd never seen a woman before. His dark eyes glowed like banked embers of a fire as they traveled slowly down her body. She felt his gaze on her like she used to feel his hands. Every nerve in her skin snapped to attention, as if reaching for the touch they remembered so well.

Mesmerized by his heated scrutiny, she couldn't move, though her pulse became erratic, her breathing rough.

Water trickled from his hair, catching in the dark stubble on his chin. She ached to run her nails across the square jaw, freeing the drops, feeling the contrast of the cool water and warm skin.

''I won!'' the boys chorused.

The spell broke into pieces. Rafe turned away. Emma took a deep, shaky breath. So much for her theory that her body would turn him off.

''I was first,'' Randy argued.

''I was,'' Gabe returned. ''Rafe, wasn't I first?''

Rafe swam to the other side. ''Sorry, guys. I didn't see who won. Want to try again?''

Emma didn't hear their reply because she made a clean dive into the pool. The cool water was a shock to her hot skin, but one she welcomed.

She surfaced on the other side in time to hear Rafe ask if they wanted to play Marco Polo. It turned out he knew lots of water games, which he said he learned from his nieces and nephews in

Houston. They played them all with the boys. Emma enjoyed herself as much as the boys, though she suspected Rafe deliberately suggested games which involved some form of touching, then ruthlessly went after her.

Or maybe she enjoyed herself because of that.

At any rate, the next time Emma glanced at the clock, nearly two hours had passed. "Gracious, it's almost seven o'clock. Way past time to go."

"Awwww," the boys chorused.

"Five more minutes," Gabe begged.

"Oh, no. You guys promised to get out as soon as I said we had to leave, remember?"

After another chorus of "Awwww," the boys swam begrudgingly toward the ladder at the far end of the pool.

Emma turned toward the side where her clothes were, then noticed Rafe was making no move to leave. "Aren't you coming?"

He shook his head as he drifted onto his back and leisurely stroked away from her. "I'm going to swim a few laps before I get out."

Her eyes narrowed. "You just want to watch me."

He grinned roguishly. "That's a perk."

"If you think—"

"I'll be there in about an hour with a couple of pizzas."

That caught her attention. "Pizzas?"

"I told your mother not to cook tonight. I'm going to pick up some pizzas. Sort of a house-warming party."

Since he turned over and started the crawl stroke in earnest, Emma couldn't argue. So she swam to the ladder by her chair and climbed out.

She watched him swim as she dried off and dressed. His strokes were clean and strong, proving his claim of swimming for fitness. But something was odd.

Suddenly it struck her. Even though the sun had dipped below the motel, throwing shade over the pool, Rafe still wore the

T-shirt. That had to be awkward, with the sodden material hampering his strokes.

Then she recalled that even though the temperatures had been spiking up into the nineties, he always wore long pants and long-sleeved shirts. That was why she hadn't seen the scars on his arms before now.

And come to think of it, he'd already been in the water when they arrived today.

He was trying to hide his scars.

Why? She'd seen the ones on his face and arms. Did he think a few more would matter?

She looked away from him, telling herself she wasn't hurt because he didn't trust her. That would certainly be the kettle calling the frying pan black. Besides, feeling hurt would mean she cared, and she didn't. She couldn't. She absolutely refused to care that much about anyone outside her family again.

She corralled the boys and dried them off for the trip home. When they were about to walk out the gate, she glanced back. Rafe cut through the water with slow, powerful strokes.

Suddenly she remembered his taste in pizzas. She walked to the end of the pool, kneeled down and tapped him on the shoulder when he touched the wall.

He threw his head up in surprise, his eyes wide. Then he grinned. "I remember. No anchovies."

"Mom! Momma! Where are you?" Gabe's cry was accompanied by his small feet stomping up the stairs to Rafe's apartment.

Rafe was being wined and dined by a printer who wanted his business, so Emma was alone at the computer. She swiveled in the chair and rose to open the door for her son. "Gracious! What is it?"

He reached the landing and stared up at her. He was still dressed in his dirt-streaked uniform. His face was flushed and his eyes brimmed with tears. "Coach is moving away, Mom. What are we gonna do?"

She reached out and pulled him inside the office. She tried to brush some of the dirt off his face, but only succeeded in mixing it with sweat to make mud streaks. "Coach is leaving? When?"

"In two weeks," Gabe told her, his bottom lip trembling. "He's been transper...transfer..."

"Transferred?"

"Yeah, that. To Dallas." He wiped his nose across his sleeve. "There's five more weeks in the season, Mom! What are we gonna do?"

"I'm sure they'll find a new coach for you to—"

"No! He told us at practice today he couldn't find anybody. He's been calling all the dads and even the moms. Everybody's too busy."

Emma pulled him into a hug. Having the T-ball season over early was the end of the world to a five-year-old.

Gabe pulled back and looked up at her hopefully. "Do you think Rafe could be our coach?"

Her hands tightened on his small shoulders. Her first instinct was to scream *No!* Gabe worshipped the ground his coach walked on. The last thing she wanted was for her son to turn Rafe into some kind of baseball-breathing hero.

As her panic receded, however, she came up with a better reason. "I don't think Rafe's up to that much exercise."

"But—"

"I've watched a couple of practices. Coach was running back and forth between the players showing them what to do."

"But—"

"Rafe can't run, Gabe. He told me so."

His dark eyes refilled with tears. "The season can't end now Mom. We haven't even won a game yet."

Her heart sank, and her own eyes filled with tears. This wasn' Gabe's first disappointment in life, and it certainly wouldn't b his last, but it was now, and he was hurting.

She pulled off his baseball cap and ran a hand back through his damp, thick hair. "Tell you what. Let me shut down the computer. Then while you take a bath, I'll call around and see what I can find out, okay?"

"Okay," he replied without much hope.

By the time Gabe was dressed for bed, Emma had some good news and some bad news for him.

The bad news was that she had talked to the coach and the director of the league. Nobody had been found to take over coaching the T-Ball Tigers.

The good news—for Gabe, at least—was that she had volunteered.

"Mom!" He stared at her as if she'd suddenly turned purple. "You don't know anything about baseball."

"I know a little. I used to play softball when I was in school. Besides, the coach said y'all pretty much know what to do by now. I just need to be there to supervise. He'll be at the game on Saturday, so your new coach will have a little bit of coaching herself." She straightened the twisted waistband of his pajamas. "Are you okay with this? If I don't take the job, you'll have to quit for the season."

Gabe leaned into her and wrapped his arms around her neck. "Thanks, Mom. I'm glad you're not like the other guys' parents. I'm glad you have time for us."

Emma returned her son's hug. Time was something she didn't have much of, either, but she would give up sleeping before she disappointed her son.

Now all she had to do was find a way to keep this news from Rafe as long as she could. Not only would he laugh at the idea of her coaching baseball, but he'd know she didn't ask him to do it because she wanted to keep him from Gabe. He'd give her that hurt/angry look he always gave her when she refused to let him do something with Gabe. The one that made her feel so guilty.

Rafe would jump at the chance to coach the team. She knew

he would. Gabe was more important to him than *Southern Yesteryears*.

But the last thing she needed was something else to magnify Rafe in her son's eyes. Gabe already thought he was a superhero. The next step up was...Dad.

Chapter Seven

"No, that's not what I want you to do."

Rafe lifted his head from the article he was editing to where Emma worked on the computer. "Pardon me?"

She looked over her shoulder sheepishly. "Sorry. I tend to talk to computers. Especially when they do what I tell them to do instead of what I want them to do."

He chuckled. "If I did that there would be a constant conversation."

"Are you still having trouble? I made it as easy as I could for you to get on and write your articles."

"I know. I'm sure one of these days I'll learn enough so it's not always beeping at me." He lifted a shoulder. "But sometimes I wish I had my dad's old typewriter."

"Is that how you've been writing?" she asked, clearly horrified.

"Yep."

She shook her head as if it was the saddest thing she'd ever heard. "You *have* been living in the Dark Ages."

Rafe rose from the desk where he'd been working and stretched. "What are you working on now?"

"I'm redoing the cover title."

He stepped over to stand behind her chair so he could see the screen. "I liked what you showed me yesterday."

She wrinkled her nose. "You've liked everything I've shown you."

"It's all good. You're good."

"The magazine that comes with our clip art service at work had a technique I want to try. Look." She clicked on a window in the background which popped forward. It contained the two words of the magazine's name. *Yesteryear* was fat and wide in outline type. *Southern* was in smaller letters spread out on top. "I rummaged through the file of old photographs you have. I'm scanning them in, colorizing them, then I'm going to paste them inside the letters."

When he looked at the screen blankly, she chuckled. "Just wait. I think you'll like it even better than what I showed you yesterday."

She clicked on the window she'd been working on, pressed some keys and the trees in the photograph that had been red turned to black and white. She clicked the mouse and pressed more keys, and a minute later the trees were green. She worked so fast she made him dizzy.

"You're coloring old black-and-white photographs? Like Ted Turner does to old movies? Why?"

"To add color to the logo. You don't want a black-and-white cover title. That's dull as dirt. Watch. I'm going to take this picture of a Civil War battlefield and paste it into the *Y* of *Yesteryears*."

She clicked and pressed more keys, then suddenly the *Y* was filled with the photograph. Somehow she maneuvered the picture around inside the letter until the best part showed through.

"There," she said. "What do you think?"

"I think I definitely hired the right graphic artist. You're amazing."

She shrugged. "It's not hard. It just takes a while to learn. But what do you think about the concept?"

"It's perfect. You're going to fill all the letters of *Yesteryears* with historical photographs, right?"

She picked up a folder and opened it. "Right. Let me show you the ones I'm planning on using."

Rafe pulled the chair from his desk and took the photographs from her as she handed them to him. "These are all historical. Battles and generals and famous people."

She frowned. "It's a history magazine, isn't it?"

"Yes, but..." He glanced up in surprise. "I guess we really haven't talked much about the concept, have we?"

She shook her head.

"I had some market research done before I made the final decision to start this venture. Surveys, focus groups, that kind of thing. I found out that women are the main purchasers of magazines. And if we want *Southern Yesteryears* to appeal to women, we've got to give them something they're interested in reading about."

"Which isn't war and generals," Emma said thoughtfully. "You mean everyday type stories. Gardening. Cooking. Decorating."

"Right. All of those things have their own unique history. If we want *Southern Yesteryears* to be as popular as *Southern Living,* we need to make it look like *Southern Living*—which is your job—and read like *Southern Living*—which is mine. We're going to have old-fashioned gardening tips. What flowers Southerners planted a hundred years ago. What they cooked. How they cooked. What kind of furniture they made and bought. And relate it to how people do those things today."

Emma leaned back in her chair. "This magazine is going to sell like beer at baseball games."

He smiled. Her prediction meant more to him than all the reports the marketing research company had supplied. "Let's hope so."

"You're brilliant."

She looked at him as if he'd just discovered a cure for aging. Suddenly he felt two stories tall. "Like I said, I did market research."

"But you had the idea."

He shrugged.

"So I need to find different kinds of pictures like an old garden gate, a cooking hearth, antiques." A faraway look glazed her eyes. "Yes. I'm going to like this even better."

"Thank you."

"For what?"

He reached across and took her hand. Because he was expecting them, the memories weren't such a shock. The ones that came now were of her helping him with story ideas, insights on stories he was working on, possible sources. "We made a good team." He studied her lovely face, which regarded him warily. "We still do."

"Don't," she whispered.

"Don't what?"

She drew her hand from his. "Don't look at me like that."

"How am I looking at you?"

"Like...like..." Crimson stained her cheeks. "Like you want to kiss me."

"I do."

She stood abruptly. "You agreed to keep our relationship strictly business."

"I know." He ran a hand through his hair. "But I can't help looking at you like I want you, because I do."

"Rafe, I—"

"I know." He pushed his chair back toward his desk. "I'm supposed to let you touch me. I forgot for a minute. I'm sorry. It won't happen again."

"That's what you said before."

His face tightened. "Is my touch so abhorrent?"

She opened her mouth to speak, then pressed her lips together. After a moment she looked away.

The look on her face told him she couldn't say yes and wouldn't say no. "Emma—"

"No!" She backed away from him. "I can't work this way, Rafe. I can't come up here every night knowing you're going to try to break down my defenses."

Defenses. The word implied having to fight against something. One part of Rafe hoped it was desire for him. Another part feared the same thing.

What was he doing? He'd promised both her and himself that he would keep their relationship strictly business.

Yet...he wanted her so damn much. He craved her touch like a drowning man craves air.

So what would he do if she touched him back? How far would his desire let her go? He'd seen her reaction at the pool when she glimpsed the scars on his arms. If she saw the rest of him...

Desolation threatened to choke him. He was twice damned— hungering for something that was already his and not being able to even touch it.

"You're right." He sat down hard in his chair. "I'm sorry. I swear I won't touch you again. From now on, I'll wait for you to touch me."

Her expression, though still guarded, relaxed somewhat. "You mean for your memories."

"Of course."

As she hesitantly sat down at the computer again, he swung back to the article on his desk and stared blindly at the typed words. He felt the connection he'd been searching for ever since he'd wakened with no memories—the connection he'd thought he'd found after all these years—drifting farther and farther out of reach.

And he didn't know what the hell to do about it.

Rafe parked on the curb next door since his usual parking place in front of the house was occupied by several large trucks.

Emma and Sylvia stood in the front yard, deep in conversation with a burly man dressed in jeans and a short-sleeved shirt. Gabe and Randy were running up the steps and jumping off the porch.

Rafe glanced at his watch. Two-fifteen. What was Emma doing home so early on a Friday afternoon?

He climbed out of his truck and saw the sign on the side of one of the trucks. River City Roofing Company. About time they showed up. They'd been promising to come all week. Emma must've taken off early to deal with them.

As he made his way up the drive, Rafe noticed the confusion on Sylvia's face, the roofer's crafty amusement and the wariness on Emma's. She stood with her arms crossed over her stomach.

When he got closer, he understood why. The roofer was explaining the procedure, using all kinds of technical jargon, but in a tone as if he were talking to a child.

Where did Emma find this guy?

Sylvia was the first to see him. Her features cleared with obvious relief. "Oh, thank goodness, there's Rafe. He's the one paying for the roof. He'll understand."

He understood all right. The man was a jerk who'd probably take advantage of these two women given half a chance. Rafe extended his hand as Emma introduced the roofer as Dennis Ford, vowing not to let the guy have the chance.

Vapid blue eyes turned to size him up as the roofer gave Rafe a bruising handshake.

"Mr. Ford was just going over a few things concerning the roof."

Rafe caught the stiffness in Emma's voice and turned to meet her gaze. He knew instantly that she understood exactly what the roofer was doing. What's more, she clearly expected Rafe to take over last-minute negotiations with the man—and already resented him for it.

"I'm sure glad you're here, Mr. Johnson," the man told him.

"Maybe you'll understand what I'm trying to tell the little lady. We're gonna have to—"

"You've got the wrong impression, Mr. Ford," Rafe told him. "I'm just a boarder. These ladies own the house. Emma's the one you need to haggle with."

"But, Rafe." Sylvia placed a hand on his arm. "You men understand these things so much better."

Rafe lifted a brow. As sweet as Sylvia was, sometimes he could see why Emma got so frustrated with her mother. He patted her hand. "Emma's an intelligent woman, Sylvia. She can understand what Mr. Ford's talking about." He turned to stab the roofer with his stare. "As long as the man speaks English. If she can't, I guess you'll just have to hire another roofer."

Mr. Ford's eyes narrowed.

"It *is* your money, Rafe," Emma said grudgingly.

He shook his head. "It's rent money. Remember? A roof over your head for a roof over mine."

Emma regarded him as if she wasn't quite certain what species he came from.

His attitude clearly surprised and confused her. Good.

"If you'll excuse me, I'm going to play ball with my—" He broke off, realizing he was about to say *son*. "With my little friends here. If you need my help, call me. Otherwise, we'll be in the backyard."

As he walked toward the porch, he felt Emma's green gaze burning into him every inch of the way.

The natives were getting restless.

Emma glanced around at thirteen boys and girls who should be looking to her for instructions. Instead, their five- and six-year-old attention spans were wandering away. Three girls were giggling together at the edge of the small crowd. A couple of boys were playing simultaneous pitch with their gloves. One boy was turned completely around, watching a dog chasing a bird across the outfield. Even Gabe and Randy were whispering together.

If she didn't think of something to occupy them in the next thirty seconds, she was going to lose control over the entire situation.

The T-Ball Tigers had already covered everything on the list the coach had given her. They'd completed their warm-up drills. Each boy and girl had taken their turn at bat. They'd tossed the ball back and forth to one another. She'd even had them run the bases several times.

Not that she'd ever had what one might call control. Keeping the attention of this many kids this age was a definite challenge, one she wasn't sure she could keep up week after week. She was exhausted. Surely the time allotted for practice was almost over.

She glanced at her watch and had to hold back a panicked moan. Thirty more minutes before the parents were due to pick them up.

To make matters even worse, Rafe had shown up at the field just after practice started. Dressed in jeans, a long-sleeved shirt and a baseball cap, he leaned against the fence just ten yards away. She wished she'd watched the team practice all these weeks instead of using the time to run errands like the other parents did. Maybe she would know what to do now.

"Um, anything y'all think we need to work on to get ready for Saturday's game?"

A hand immediately went up. Arthur. The smartest kid but the worst player on the team. He'd probably be a rocket scientist one day.

"Yes, Arthur?"

"How about pitching to us?"

"Pitch?" She cleared her throat and lowered her voice below a squeak. On the plus side, Arthur's suggestion had reclaimed the attention of the entire team. "You mean throw the ball so you can hit it?"

They all nodded.

She shook her head. "This is T-ball. You hit the ball off the T, remember?"

"The coach is supposed to pitch to his team the last couple of weeks of the season." Arthur pushed his glasses up his nose. "That's just two weeks away."

One of the girls pushed Arthur's arm. "*Her* team, dummy."

Arthur started to push back, but Emma quickly stepped between them. "We're supposed to be having fun, remember?"

The two nodded reluctantly.

"Are y'all sure about this pitching thing? Coach didn't mention it."

They all started talking at once. From the gist of what she could understand, they all knew about the pitching at the end of the season.

Great. Emma had never pitched a baseball in her life. When she'd played, way back when, she'd been an outfielder who had to throw the ball with more strength than finesse.

But she'd try anything to keep the kids occupied for another thirty minutes. How hard could it be?

"Okay, then. Y'all take your places on the field."

Aware the whole time of Rafe's eyes on her, Emma picked up the ball and walked out to the mound. Randy was the first batter.

"You ready?" she called.

He nodded and posed himself with the bat the way she'd seen players do on television.

Taking a deep breath, Emma pitched the ball.

The entire team erupted in protests as the ball sailed several feet over Randy's head.

"Not underhand, Mom," Gabe called from first base. "That's for girls."

The girls within hearing distance glared at Gabe.

Emma lifted her arms helplessly. "How, then?"

Gabe ran over to the pitcher's mound. He took the ball and without releasing it, showed her how to pitch.

Emma swallowed hard. Overhand looked even harder than underhand. "Did Coach teach you that?"

Gabe shook his head. "Rafe did."

"Rafe knows how to pitch?" She glanced to where he leaned against the fence. He hadn't said a word the whole time, hadn't even cracked a smile, though he had to be laughing at her total lack of coaching ability.

Gabe looked at him, too. "Maybe Rafe could pitch for us."

She frowned. "I thought you said the coach had to do it."

Her son didn't say anything, but his thoughts were clear as he regarded her solemnly.

Emma took a deep breath. Turning the coaching job over to Rafe would probably be the best thing she could do for the kids. She certainly wasn't any good at it. She wasn't doing much more than baby-sitting the team so they could play out the season. Rafe could probably help them become better players.

Could he handle the job, physically? Probably. The running back and forth she'd done was mostly because she didn't have a clue as to what she was doing.

But was she ready to see Gabe's growing affection for Rafe increase even more? They already spent more time together than she liked. Rafe was home all day. Though he worked on the magazine, he made time to spend with his son—with her mother's help and blessing, she suspected. At least Randy was there during the day, so they weren't alone.

On the other hand, could she disappoint the whole team just to keep her son's love all to herself? Rafe was Gabe's father. She was going to have to tell her son—soon. She had to learn to handle Gabe's love for his father sooner or later. She might as well start getting used to it.

Turning to the team, she called, "Five-minute break." Then she walked over to Rafe.

He pulled off his sunglasses and watched her approach.

She stopped several feet short of the fence. "They've taken a vote. They want you to coach. Do you want the job?"

He adjusted the baseball cap on his head. "I got the feeling this past week you didn't trust me to be Gabe's coach."

Her eyes dropped to his shirt-clad arms crossed on top of the fence. She should've known he'd pick up on her misgivings. He was proving damnably good at reading her, just like he used to be.

"Have you changed your mind?"

She pressed her lips together and searched his eyes. Though they were dark, the soul behind them wasn't. He'd kept his word about not touching her while they worked, though she sometimes caught a look of longing on his face. He'd also kept his word about not telling Gabe he was his father.

"I'm a lousy coach," she said. "And I can't pitch. The kids need you."

He didn't move. "You didn't answer the question."

Damn the man. Why did he always have to push?

"Do you want the job or not?" she asked.

"Not unless you trust me not to do whatever it was you were afraid I was going to do."

She wanted to cross her arms over her stomach, but knew the body language would belie the words she had to utter. Could she actually say the word *trust?* It hadn't been in her vocabulary for such a long, long time. "I do."

"You do what?"

"Trust you." She squeezed the ball in her hand so hard she thought it might bust a seam. Then she added, "To coach the T-ball team."

He lifted a brow. "I guess that's a start."

She held out the ball.

His eyes didn't leave hers. "I want you to know that I didn't come today to take over. I came because my son wanted me to watch."

"All right."

"I'm not Borg, Emma."

She frowned. "I suppose Momma told you about that."

He shrugged. "Do you understand?"

"Yes." She took a step closer and handed him the ball. "You're not taking control. I'm giving it to you."

His smile made her knees threaten to buckle. "I'll take the job on one condition."

She rolled her eyes. "What?"

"You coach with me."

She frowned and tossed a hand to where kids ran around the infield like zoo animals that had just been released from their cages. "You've seen how good I am at this."

He shrugged. "I need you, Emma. I may have the know-how, but I don't have the legs. I can tell them how to chase down a ball, but I can't show them how to do it. You can. Together we can do it."

She held his gaze for a long moment, both hoping and fearing to find the meaning she heard in his words. Finally she said softly, "Okay."

His smile deepened the lines around his eyes. He tossed the ball in the air and caught it with a snap of his wrist, then limped around the fence and called, "Let's play ball!"

Emma didn't glance up from the computer when Rafe pushed the apartment door open. After he spent several minutes whistling as he stood in various points around the room, however, her curiosity got the best of her.

She swiveled around to see him with a hammer in one hand and a frame in the other. He was holding the frame against the wall, as if judging how it would look.

"What are you hanging?" she asked.

He cocked his head. "A picture. How does it look here?"

She finally stood. "How can I say, when I don't even—"

She stopped abruptly as she saw what he'd framed. It was the angel picture she'd drawn years ago. The lined yellow paper, worn and dirty, was made even dingier by the gold-painted wood of the new frame.

She folded her arms across her stomach. "Why did you waste your money on that old thing?"

"This 'old thing' means a lot to me." He handed it to her,

then drew a nail from his shirt pocket. "It's about time I protected it, instead of carrying it around in my wallet."

As he pounded in the nail, Emma stared down at the lines she'd drawn so long ago while daydreaming about her lover. Though cartoonish, she'd captured the contrast of Rafe's rakish expression on an angel's body.

The picture meaning so much to him that he'd go to the trouble and expense of getting it framed shouldn't mean so much to her. It shouldn't make her feel breathless or cause her heart to ache. But it did.

Rafe reached for the frame, and Emma laid it in his hand without meeting his eyes, then returned to the computer.

"'...I will myself tell the name of the knight whose lance occasioned my falling: it was the Knight of Ivanhoe; nor was there—'"

"He's asleep."

Emma's quiet comment brought Rafe out of twelfth-century England to find her green eyes on him. He glanced down at Gabe, who'd nodded off, curled against his side.

Moved beyond words at the innocent, trusting warmth of his son, Rafe smoothed back a lock of Gabe's dark hair. Believing for so long he'd never have moments like this made each one infinitely precious.

"I'm boring him," he said without taking his eyes off his son. "I've been paraphrasing most of the description, but I guess he's just too young for this now."

"He loved every minute of it," Emma assured him. "But it's an hour past his bedtime."

Rafe smiled at her ruefully. She'd swiveled around from the computer, and he wondered how long she'd been watching him. "Sorry. I tend to get caught up in the story."

Her mouth quirked. "Really?"

He glanced down at the dog-eared, well-worn copy. "My mother said it was my favorite book when I was a boy. I've read it several times while I was...incapacitated. Thanks for letting me share it with Gabe.''

"I'm not a monster, Rafe."

He met her gaze steadily. "I know."

"Do you? One could think you're reading that particular story as an object lesson."

"An object lesson? What does that mean?"

"*Ivanhoe* is a story about a man who comes back from the dead and has to prove himself so his family will accept him. You don't see the parallels between Ivanhoe and yourself?"

He hadn't. The fact that she'd seen them caused several emotions to hit Rafe in rapid succession. First came delighted surprise at the quick workings of her mind. He'd discovered her intelligence in the weeks they'd been together, and it turned him on.

Hope rapidly built on the surprise. Her insight proved she thought about him, which turned him on even more.

Frustration won the round, however, because he realized they were back to the point where she was reading something into everything he did.

Damn it. What the hell had he done now? For the past week, they'd been getting along better than he'd expected to by this time. He'd believed he was making progress, that she was beginning to trust him. She'd let him coach the T-Ball Tigers, and tonight she'd let him read Gabe his bedtime story.

Now he felt like he'd barely taken one step forward before she shoved him two steps back.

"Ivanhoe had to prove he didn't betray the king," he said softly. "What do I have to prove?"

She crossed her arms over her stomach—a sure sign she didn't want to answer—and stood. "I need to put Gabe to bed."

When she stepped over to pick Gabe up, Rafe rose and stretched Gabe out on the couch.

"What are you doing?" Emma whispered roughly. "I said I'm taking him to bed."

"Not yet, you're not." He covered the boy with an afghan

Sylvia had provided. "You brought this subject up, and we're going to finish it. But not where we can disturb Gabe."

He straightened and gestured toward the door. "After you."

She lifted her chin and pressed her lips together. Just when he was about to drag her outside she moved—with obvious reluctance—out the door.

On the small landing, she wheeled to face him. "Now what?"

He pulled the door to. "I asked you a question. I expect—and deserve—an answer. What is it I have to prove to you? That I didn't betray you?"

She dropped her gaze and stared so hard at a spot on his chest he thought she wasn't going to answer. Finally she spun around to lean against the flat board railing. "I don't know."

"Then how will you know when I've done it? How will I know?"

"I don't know."

He stepped up beside her. "That's a cop-out."

She pounded her fists on the railing. "What do you want from me?"

"You know exactly what I want. I want my son. I want a family. I want..." He reached for her arm, but stopped short of touching her. "I want you to trust me. I want a chance."

Emma winced and turned to stare at the branch of the pin oak tree she could touch if she just reached out. But she didn't reach for it, just like she didn't reach for Rafe. She hadn't touched him in over a week—since the day he promised to keep his hands off her—even though there'd been a hundred times when she'd wanted to. She wanted to now. But the branch seemed so far away, and she was afraid of falling.

"You want me to prove I won't ever betray you, don't you?" he asked.

She pressed her lips together so hard they hurt. That's exactly what she wanted—to know that if she reached out, she wouldn't fall.

"That's an impossible task, *querida*. Even Ivanhoe only had to prove he didn't do something in the past, not that he wouldn't do it in the future. I can promise I won't hurt you, but I can't prove it. Only time can do that.''

Querida. It seemed like another lifetime when she'd heard him call her that. Her insides used to melt every time he used the endearment which could mean anything from ''dear one'' to ''beloved.'' Now they went up in flames.

''I know,'' she told him, her voice cracking. ''I just...''

''Just what?''

''What do you want me to do?''

''I want you to trust me not to hurt you.''

''I don't know if I can.''

He sighed heavily. ''You can try, can't you?''

''How?''

''Stop thinking of me as the enemy. I'm not here to take Gabe away from you. I'm not here to take over your life. I just want to share it.''

Hesitantly she turned and searched his eyes in the porch light. How was it possible to feel someone else's pain so clearly, so deeply? Or was his hurt just an echo of her own?

She wanted to give him everything he asked for—and more. She wanted to give him the world. But she'd reached out so many times in the past, and every time a piece of herself had gone missing. She was afraid that if she reached out one more time, there wouldn't be anything of Emma Grey left.

''Take a chance, *querida,*'' he whispered, stepping so close she could feel his heat, smell his musky warmth. But he didn't touch her. ''Take a chance on me. I won't hurt you. I swear it. How can I, when you've given me so much?''

She wanted to believe him more than she wanted her heart to take its next beat. But the very strength of her desire frightened her. Trusting him meant risking her heart, meant caring for someone she had no control over.

On the other hand...

It also meant living again. It brought hope back into the picture. Hope for the joy she'd once known with him. Hope for love.

All she had to do was reach out her hand. Such a small step, really. One she could pull back from anytime. Surely she could handle that much.

Slowly she lifted one trembling hand and placed it on his chest. The muscle jumped beneath her palm.

He sucked in a breath and closed his eyes as memories assailed him.

Emma barely noticed, because she was assailed by memories of her own. But her memories weren't of the confident, cocky, *whole* young man he'd been. She remembered Rafe from the past few weeks, how patiently he'd waited for her to touch him, to help him regain the parts of himself that he'd lost. She'd turned away from every pleading glance.

She'd done it to protect herself, but now she knew her selfishness hadn't worked. He was getting to her. She could tell by how happy it made her to make him so happy.

Alarmed, she began to withdraw her hand, but he caught it against his chest, pressing it next to his heart. His eyes opened and burned her like smoldering coals. With infinite care he brought her fingers to his lips.

"Thank you, *querida*. You won't be sorry."

She hoped to heaven he was right.

Rafe gently closed the door to his sleeping son's room. Over the past few nights, they'd gotten into the habit of tucking Gabe into bed together. After Gabe spent an hour or so with them in Rafe's apartment, Rafe carried him across the drive to the main house and into the room Gabe and Emma still shared. Rafe relished these hours the three of them spent together as a family. There were times when he forgot they weren't one.

He glanced down at Emma. "You want to go back to work?"

She nodded, but yawned as she did. "I need to finish laying out the article on pie safes."

"You look tired. Why don't you—"

She shook her head and started down the hall. "You're going to Atlanta next week to talk Coca-Cola into advertising, and you need to show them as much of the magazine as you can. Besides, it's only nine o'clock."

"You two going back over to Rafe's place?"

They turned to see Sylvia poking her head out of the living room door. While they worked at night, she caught up on the soaps she recorded during the day.

"Yes, ma'am," Rafe said.

"That's fine. Rafe, Mrs. Martin called a few minutes ago. Said she lost your number. Little Jessica's sick and won't be playing tomorrow."

"Thanks, Sylvia."

Sylvia nodded and returned to the living room.

"That's too bad," Rafe said as he opened the back door for Emma. "Jessica catches the ball better than anyone on the team except for Gabe and Randy."

Emma threw him a rueful smile. "She talks better than anyone on the team, too."

He chuckled. "If we could just, with a clear conscience, teach her to talk trash to the other team, we'd have ourselves the perfect little shortstop."

They stepped out into the humid night air. Cicadas and crickets played their wing songs from the trees and grass, and the smell of wisteria climbing up the trellis on the wall perfumed the whole yard.

Emma brought a bunch of the grapelike flowers to her nose and inhaled deeply. "Mmm. Wisteria smells best at night."

"It's beautiful," he said, never taking his eyes from her profile.

"This vine has been growing here all of my life." She turned to look at him. "Do you remember it?"

He shook his head.

She reached her hand out hesitantly, then drew it back.

"What's wrong?" he asked softly.

Her hand clenched into a fist. "I...is it okay to touch you?"

His heart gunned like a car engine under a teenager's heavy foot. "*Querida,* you can touch me anytime you like. Any*where* you like."

She sucked in a quick breath, then slowly extended her hand and laid it on his chest.

"Are you crazy?" Emma whispered from her window above him.

Rafe grinned as he reached up for another handhold on the trellis. "Crazy about you."

"Shhh! My father will wake up and kill you—if you don't fall and kill yourself."

A minute later he was at her window.

She leaned out and caressed his cheek. "We can't make love tonight. My father is just down the hall. He'll hear us."

"All I want is a kiss."

"Just one kiss?"

"Just one. Then I'll go."

"You are crazy," she breathed, then touched her lips to his.

Rafe focused on the green eyes that watched him with wonder. "We played Romeo and Juliet."

"I couldn't believe you climbed up there just to give me a kiss," she whispered.

"You fussed at me for weeks after that."

She smiled crookedly. Her voice was husky as she said, "I thought you were the craziest, handsomest, most heroic and romantic man I'd ever met."

"And now?"

"Now?" She frowned and backed away. "Now I have work to do."

He watched as she spun and all but ran up the steps to his apartment.

"Coward," he whispered. But he didn't know if he was talking to her or to himself.

Chapter Eight

"These peaches are heavenly." They were the first peaches of the summer, and Emma refused to feel guilty as she scooped more of the sugared fruit into her bowl. "Did you get them at the farmers' market?"

Sylvia shook her head. "Rafe brought them in."

Emma glanced across the table. "I forgot. You were always crazy about peaches. Where'd you find them? Someone selling them on the side of the road?"

Rafe shook his head. "Jay brought them to me. He and his family went canoeing in Arkansas this past weekend."

Emma hesitated with her spoon halfway to her mouth. "Jay came to see you again?"

"This afternoon."

She frowned. "That's the third time in a week. I guess he wanted the same old thing?"

"Yes." Rafe smiled ruefully across the table. "This time he made me an offer I couldn't refuse."

Suddenly her appetite for peaches vanished. Her spoon clattered as she dropped it into her bowl. "You're going back to work for the paper?"

"Not really." He scraped the last bit of juice from his second helping. "Just freelance. I'm going to write an article on Memphis history twice a month for the Sunday issue."

Her eyes narrowed. "He thinks if he can squeeze your foot in the door, he can drag you all the way in."

Rafe shrugged. "He can think what he likes. I agreed because I thought it'd be a great way to get my name out there to promote *Southern Yesteryears.*"

"I see," Emma murmured. Though she'd averted her eyes, she could feel his gaze on her.

"What's wrong?" he asked.

"Nothing." She stood suddenly and picked up her dishes. "Time to clean up the kitchen."

Rafe pushed his chair back. "I'll help."

"Don't trouble yourself," Sylvia told him. "We can handle this."

"Yes." Emma stopped at the swinging door, glad she'd dismissed her son from the table five minutes earlier. For some reason Rafe's news had felt like a punch in her gut, and she needed time to figure out why. The mindless task of cleaning up the supper dishes was perfect for thinking, but only if she did it alone. She'd already discovered, much to her chagrin, that she didn't do a lot of productive thinking when Rafe was close by. "Gabe's probably already back with Randy. I'm sure they're waiting for you to hit them some grounders like you promised."

He shrugged. "They can wait."

"No." When Emma's sharp tone made him raise a brow at her, she added, "Please. The boys need someone watching them."

He raised his hands in surrender. "Fine. Far be it from me to interfere with women's work."

Relieved, Emma ignored his sarcasm and pushed her way into the kitchen. Her mother helped clear the table, then she shooed Sylvia into the living room to start watching her soaps.

Twenty minutes later, Emma had finished loading the dish-

washer and was filling the sink with hot, soapy water to wipe
down the cabinets. She'd just about convinced herself that the
reason she was upset was that if Rafe went back to the newspaper, he'd forget all about *Southern Yesteryears* and she'd lose
the job she'd come to love. She'd been hoping that after a few
issues went on the stands, Rafe would offer her a full-time job
as production supervisor.

Then he stepped into view, framed by the window looking into
the backyard.

With her rubber-gloved hands sunk deep in hot water, she
froze, eating up his tall, lean, well-muscled form with her eyes.

Who was she kidding? She was afraid of losing Rafe...again.

Damn it! This wasn't supposed to happen. She wasn't supposed to fall in love with him again. She was supposed to protect
her heart, to keep her relationship with him all business.

But keeping Rafe out of her heart had been about as easy as
stopping a tidal wave with her bare hands. For the past six years
she'd believed a person made his or her own fate through hard
work and sacrifice. Now...

She was beginning to think Rafe was right when he said there
was some primal connection that had drawn them back together
even though they hadn't known each other was alive.

She felt the connection in countless ways: she knew without
looking that he'd walked into a room; she wanted to touch him
whenever he was around, as if the connection was so magnetic
it physically drew them together; he always seemed to know what
she was thinking.

Rafe's uneven gait took him out of sight again, and her eyes
dropped to the sponge she was squeezing.

She was falling in love with him again. How could she have
let this happen? And what the heck was she going to do about
it?

She sighed, knowing there was no way to prevent it. All she
could do now was damage control.

Okay. The main reason loving him scared her was she didn't

want him returning to the dangerous assignments he'd loved so much before, right? So she had to find some way to keep him with her. As long as they were working together on *Southern Yesteryears*, he'd be safe.

Emma thought about ways to convince him to stay in Memphis as she finished cleaning the kitchen, then went to Rafe's apartment to work on the magazine.

Rafe joined her an hour later. Randy had gone home, and Gabe went in to have his bath. Without a word, Rafe sat down at his desk and pulled out a file. He was leaving for Atlanta the next day, to convince Coca-Cola to advertise in *Southern Yesteryears*. Emma was certain he'd succeed. After all, Coca-Cola was itself part of Southern history.

As he shuffled papers, she stared at the ad for antique guns on her computer screen. The air in the room seemed electric, just because he was there.

Taking a deep breath, she pressed the keys to save the file, then swiveled around. If she wanted him to stay, she had to give him something to stay for. She had to show him that she was enough to keep him happy for the rest of his life. She had to give him the one thing she knew he wanted.

"Rafe?"

He looked over his shoulder with surprise, probably at the huskiness in her voice. "Yes?"

"I was wondering—" she cleared her throat "—if you wanted me to touch you."

He froze except for the widening of his eyes. She froze, too. This was the first friendly overture she'd made toward him. Though he'd given her every reason to believe he'd welcome her touch anytime, she couldn't help but be apprehensive.

"Like I told you." His voice was deeper than usual. "Anytime. Anywhere."

Her heart pounding like the roofers' hammers, she slowly rolled her chair closer to his, then hesitantly reached out her hand.

He met her halfway, his warm, strong fingers closing around hers.

She watched his face relax as he went back in time.

"What are you remembering?" she asked.

"The times we spent at my apartment on the river." He smiled lazily. "You're as good a cook as your mother."

Suddenly something occurred to her. What if he was falling in love with the nineteen-year-old Emma, not the woman she was today?

That was a very real possibility. She'd done everything she could to prevent him from falling in love with her and nothing to make him love her. She'd better put her plan in motion without delay—make him focus on the woman she was, not the girl who no longer existed.

"Anything else?" she asked.

His eyes focused on her face. "Actually, I'm beginning to get repeats. I guess I've remembered just about everything there is to remember."

"About us," she clarified with a frown. "You don't remember anything about your life before we met, do you?"

He shook his head. "Your magic extends only to the time we were together."

Relieved, she didn't notice he was rolling her closer until her knee slid alongside his. Her first reaction was panic. "What are you doing?"

He stopped immediately, but didn't let go of her hand. "I want to touch you back, Emma. I want to kiss you."

She inhaled quickly. This was exactly what she needed to do. She had to let down her defenses and let him get close. It was the only way to keep him with her, the only way to keep him safe. And, God help her, she wanted to feel his lips on hers.

"All right," she whispered.

His face tightened and his eyes burned into hers. She wanted to look away from their intensity, but she couldn't.

He grabbed the seat of her chair and pulled it beside his,

though turned around, making their modern office chairs into an old-fashioned love seat. Emma wrapped her arms around his neck as he encircled her waist and pulled her against him.

He closed his eyes, as if he were again seized by the past.

Frowning, she dug her fingers into his hair. "I'm here, Rafe. I'm not a memory."

His eyes opened, searing her with their heat. "Believe me, I'm aware of that. Every inch of me knows you're here."

"I thought you wanted to kiss me."

"I fully intend to." He traced her cheekbone with his fingers. "It's just that I've got you where I've wanted you ever since we kissed in my truck. Hell, ever since you walked into that damned conference room. I want to savor the moment."

"Savor this instead..." She leaned forward and touched her lips to his.

The world exploded inside her head, leaving only the reality of his arms tightening around her, his mouth drawing the very breath from her lungs. He held on until she was about to faint from lack of oxygen.

"Damn, Emma," he breathed when he pulled back a scant inch. "This is a helluva lot better than any memory. Let me in."

Joy spread through her. Her plan was working. Willingly she opened her mouth to his questing tongue, inviting him in with her own. Her blood went up in flames, blazing through her body, making her bones melt against him.

With a rough curse, he scooped her out of her chair and thrust it away with one foot. He dragged her onto his lap, settling her over the rock-hard ridge of his desire.

Emma whimpered. She vividly remembered the pleasure he could give her. This was her husband, her long-lost lover. She would recognize him if she were blind, deaf and dumb. He smelled the same. He tasted the same.

It had been so long. So long.

She wiggled closer.

With a groan Rafe leaned her back against his arm and took

the weight of her breast in his hand. She arched against the exquisite pleasure, and his mouth left hers to trail down her throat. She gripped his biceps, reveling in the strength she felt flexing beneath her fingers.

Suddenly his hand left her breast to grip her chin. "Look at me."

She opened her eyes to see him inches above her, his fierce desire making his face hard as stone.

"Tell me you want me as much as I want you."

His passion frightened her, yet at the same time made her want to crawl inside of him and never come out. "I—"

"Mom? Rafe? Y'all up here?"

Gabe's distant call made them freeze.

"Damn."

They echoed the sentiment together, then shared an uncertain smile.

"I wish I could say we'll finish this later." Rafe pushed a strand of hair off her face. "But I think we'd better take this a bit slower."

Emma sat up, telling herself she wasn't disappointed. "You're right. I never intended for it to go so far."

He smiled ruefully. "You forgot you're dealing with someone as randy as a teenager. If we make love, it will be my first time, for all practical purposes."

Emma blinked. She'd never thought of it that way. Amazed at the phenomenal control he possessed if he'd been dealing with those kinds of urges, she stood to open the door for her son.

Thank God Gabe interrupted them. If he hadn't, they'd have probably ended up in bed before they knew what happened.

As she watched her son climb on to Rafe's lap for another chapter of *Ivanhoe*, she realized that was exactly where she wanted to end up.

What better way to show him that the woman in his arms was far more desirable than the girl in his memories?

* * *

Two nights later Rafe climbed the stairs quicker than he ever had. Though it was almost midnight, the light was burning in his apartment. He hoped Emma was waiting for him.

When he turned the knob, he knew she was. The door was unlocked—something he should get onto her about. But at the moment he was too elated to care.

He pushed open the door. "Emma?"

Frowning when he got no answer, he set his garment bag on the floor and stepped into the room that served as the office. From the feel of the warm, stuffy air, the air conditioner had been off for hours. Whenever she worked up here alone, Emma switched it off.

Two steps more and he saw her, asleep on the couch.

Relief relaxed him, and his smile returned as he knelt beside her. She lay curled on her side, her head resting on one of the brocade pillows Sylvia had provided. She looked so young and innocent, like the Emma in his memories.

He pushed a strand of blond hair off her cheek. "I'm home."

Home. It really did seem like he'd come home. But home wasn't the apartment, it was this woman. In a few short weeks he felt like he belonged. That hadn't happened in all the years he'd spent in Houston.

She murmured something and burrowed deeper into the pillow.

"Wake up, *querida.* I want to kiss you."

Her lashes fluttered and her eyes opened. He watched with fascination as her eyes turned from a murky green to the bright hue of spring leaves. He realized then that he didn't know everything about their past. He just remembered they'd never wakened together. They didn't dare go to sleep back then for fear Emma would miss her curfew and be grounded. They didn't want anything to interfere with them being together.

His smile softened as he realized he still had a lot to learn about this woman who was becoming more important to him every day. He was definitely looking forward to it.

When Emma's eyes focused, she smiled sleepily. He'd never seen anything so sexy in his life.

"You're home. What time is it?" She placed her hand over a yawn.

"Almost midnight," he replied. "It was raining in Atlanta, and my flight was delayed a couple of hours."

"How did it go? Did you get the account?"

He nodded. "They've committed for a year."

She frowned. "Just a year?"

"A year is good. With a new publication, most advertisers go on a month-to-month basis until it gets established."

She relaxed. "Oh."

"They seemed very excited about the concept, and especially loved the prototype. I told them I had the best graphic designer in Memphis."

Smiling, she reached out and placed her hand on his cheek, her thumb tracing the jagged line running down his cheek. Though he was glad she touched him without hesitation, the muscle jerked reflexively. Somehow he managed not to pull away. He was glad, because her next words proved she wasn't turned off by his disfigured face.

"I missed you."

His breath caught, and he leaned close to slide an arm around her waist. While he was away, he'd convinced himself he'd dreamed the passionate episode the night before he left. He was very glad to know he hadn't. "You did?"

"Why didn't you call?"

"I didn't get in until very late last night. The advertising manager was so excited about the idea that he took me out to dinner. He even had some ideas for stories."

She smiled crookedly. "Which you'll use, of course."

He smiled back. "Of course. But not just because he's an advertiser. They were good ideas."

They smiled at each other for several minutes. Finally she said in a slightly exasperated voice, "I thought you wanted to kiss me."

Though his heart soared like the jet he'd so recently flown on, he hesitated. It was late and they were alone, not likely to be interrupted. He knew if he began kissing her, he'd want to carry her into the bedroom and stretch her out, naked, on his king-size bed. But then he'd have to get naked, too.

He shuddered, torn by self-loathing and pounding desire for the woman in his arms.

"What's wrong?" she asked hesitantly.

He traced a finger across her lower lip. "I'm afraid if I kiss you, I won't want to stop."

She shivered. "And that would be bad because...?"

"I thought we agreed to take it slow."

"I see." Her smile faded and she pushed herself up on one arm. "My mistake. I thought you wanted me."

He grabbed her hands and drew her to her feet, then pressed her against the evidence of his desire. "Tell me I don't want you."

She wound her arms around his neck. "Then kiss me."

He obliged willingly. As long as he could keep them on their feet, he'd be okay. He wouldn't have to bare his body and lose her forever. He could at least have this much of her.

Even so, the passion spiked so quickly he nearly lost control. Only when he'd reached under her sweater to unhook her bra did alarms go off in his head.

He released the elastic reluctantly and dropped her light sweater back into place. He held her close until her breathing eased.

"You stopped."

He kissed the top of her head. "I...want you to be absolutely sure this is what you want."

She leaned back in his arms to look up at him. "You kept pushing me until I finally realized I wanted you. Now you're the one pulling away."

"I never pushed you."

She backed out of his arms. "Maybe not overtly, but you always looked at me as if you wanted me."

"I did," he told her. "I still do."

"Then why did you stop?"

He couldn't believe he was actually talking her out of making love. He'd dreamed about having her in his bed for nearly a month. Maybe if he turned out the lights...

No. The scars would still be there for her to feel, which would probably be even more of a shock than seeing them.

"I told you, I want you to be sure. You just decided three days ago to trust me. Let's give it a little time."

"How much time?"

He met her eyes squarely. "Until you can trust me enough to tell Gabe he's my son."

She looked away guiltily, and he knew he was safe for a while. Part of him was relieved, and part wanted to howl in frustration.

He grabbed her hand. "Come on. I'll walk you to your room."

They'd moved back upstairs after the roofers had finished two days before. Rafe escorted her to the room at the back corner of the house—the room separated from his by only twenty yards of grass and concrete. At the moment it felt like light-years away.

He kissed her lips. "Go to sleep. We've got a game tomorrow."

She nodded and disappeared into her room.

He descended the stairs, locked the back door, then climbed to his apartment. He turned off the light in the office, then caught sight of her light through the open curtains. He limped over to the window.

She'd left her curtains open, too. Probably forgot to close them. Not that it mattered. The carriage house and thick oak trees blocked any neighbor's view into her room. No one could see inside. No one but him.

As he watched, she passed in front of the window, pulling her sweater off over her head.

Every muscle in his body tightened with the need to forget himself inside her, to make her his. Knowing she wanted him, too, made staying in place the hardest thing he could remember doing.

Stiff-armed, he leaned against the jamb and took deep breaths, trying to cool his heated blood. It didn't work.

He was beginning to believe that nothing would. Ever.

Pandemonium reigned in the private room at the back of the pizza parlor. The T-Ball Tigers and their parents had commandeered the entire room to celebrate the victory that morning. The kids were flying high because it was their first win, helped along by pizza and soft drinks.

Emma sat at a corner table with Randy's mother, watching Rafe play video games with Gabe. They'd dropped Sylvia off at the house after the game because she had plans to lunch with friends.

"I'm glad you were there today," Emma said to Audra Jenkins, who watched her own husband play video games with her son. "It means a lot to Randy."

"It meant a lot to us, too. Seeing him make the game-winning hit was better than putting a hundred felons in jail."

Five-foot-seven with auburn hair, blue eyes and the figure of a model, Audra looked every inch the prosecuting attorney. The Jenkinses had to work on most Saturdays, but they loved Randy, and that was what counted in Emma's book.

"We're not supposed to win, really. At this age, they're supposed to play for fun. We're supposed to make every effort to have a tie game, which we've done all season." Emma smiled wryly. "But the team today looked as if they couldn't have caught beach balls."

Audra shook her head as she stirred her soft drink with a straw. "It's more than the other team being so bad. Randy tells me how much Rafe has been helping him and Gabe. Throwing to them, pitching. I can see how much Randy's improved since the game I saw earlier in the season."

"Rafe plays with the boys every day when he's in town. He loves it as much as they do, I think."

"He's starting a magazine, right?"

Emma told her about working on *Southern Yesteryears,* then Audra shared anecdotes about some of her cases. They didn't talk much on a regular basis. Since they both had full-time jobs and families, they were always too busy for chitchat. But Emma enjoyed the times they did.

When the group began breaking up, Arthur's mother called for everyone's attention.

"I want to get a picture of the players," Mrs. Cook announced. "Everyone line up on this wall with the coaches."

The kids ran, skipped or jumped to the wall where Mrs. Cook arranged them. Gabe pulled Rafe over. Rafe bent to say something to Gabe, who then ran over to get her.

"That's it," Mrs. Cook said as she saw Emma coming. "Stand there on the left side of the kids, Emma. Rafe, you stand on the right. Gabe, why don't you stand next to your father?"

"Huh?" Gabe gaped at Mrs. Cook. "Rafe? He's not my dad."

"Oh." Arthur's mom looked hard at the two of them. "Well, bless me. You're the spittin' image. Oh, well. Stand next to your coach, then."

Rafe met Emma's eyes across the double row of kids. His thoughts were clear. He wanted to shout to the world that Gabe was his son.

Emma knew she had to give in soon, but this certainly wasn't the time or place. Gabe needed to be told in private.

She tore her gaze away. She couldn't even say what it was that held her back. Only that she couldn't bring herself to say the words.

But the way her son was looking thoughtfully at his father, it needed to be soon.

"Hold still, everybody!" Mrs. Cook called. "Say cheese!"

* * *

Emma stretched as she entered her bedroom, reveling in the luxury of having a room all to herself again.

Without turning on the light, she wandered to the window overlooking the back of the house, the one directly across from Rafe's apartment. The furniture was in exactly the same place it had been all her life, so she knew the way by heart.

It had been a long day but a good one. After they'd left the pizza parlor, Rafe had taken her and Gabe to a movie, then to supper. When they finally got home, Gabe was so tired they barely got him bathed before he fell asleep.

Emma hadn't gotten a lick of work done today, but she didn't care. Which was odd. Usually she counted the success of her days by how much she got done. She scheduled her hours closely, making certain she had enough to fill them, making certain she didn't have enough time to think about how empty she felt inside.

She hadn't known that was what she was doing until Rafe came back into her life. She'd thought her life was full enough with the love she shared with Gabe and her mother. She'd refused to admit there'd been a gaping hole inside her that only one man could fill—that man being Rafe.

Taking a whole day to play had been a good sign. It showed she didn't feel empty anymore. She'd needed a day like today. She hadn't known how much until she had it.

Rafe knew. Whenever she'd mentioned getting back to clean the house, he'd whisked them off someplace else.

Emma rubbed the fingers of one hand across her lips. They were still raw from thanking him. She hadn't wanted to let him go tonight. She'd longed to follow him up to his apartment, fall with him onto his king-size bed and see if he could make her feel the way he used to make her feel—infinitely precious, boundlessly loved, every inch female.

She hadn't even suggested it. She still wasn't ready to tell Gabe that Rafe was his father.

She wanted to trust Rafe, but though she was ninety-nine percent sure he wasn't going to be lured back to the newspaper, there was still a niggling doubt. Besides, how was she supposed to tell her son she'd lied to him all these years? How did one explain to a five-year-old the intricacies of a forbidden love, or the complex webs woven when you tried too hard to keep your place in society?

She leaned her head against the windowpane and wondered which side of her would win—her sexual frustration or the long habits of distrust.

As the glass cooled her skin, she suddenly noticed something odd about Rafe's apartment. The lights weren't on.

She straightened. It had been at least five minutes since he'd left. He should be there by now.

Her heart accelerated. What if he'd fallen on the steps? He had to be as tired as she was, and with his injuries...

She whirled and flew down the stairs. She cursed as she fumbled with the lock on the back door, but finally shoved it open and raced down the path. Relieved he wasn't sprawled at the bottom of the steps, she bolted up them and threw open his unlocked door.

"Rafe?"

"What is it?" he asked in alarm.

"Where are you?"

"In here."

His voice led her into the office, where she saw him silhouetted against the light of the window, rising from the chair that had been turned to face outward.

"What's wrong?" he asked.

"That's what I came to ask you." She stepped farther into the room. "Why haven't you turned on a light? You aren't sick, are you?"

He uttered a muffled curse in Spanish, then said, "No."

"What are you doing?"

He shook his head, but his voice sounded amused as he said, "I refuse to answer that on the grounds I might be arrested."

Her brow wrinkled. "What?"

He sighed loudly and held out his hand. "Come here. I'll show you."

She approached cautiously, uncertain of his mood. When she reached him, he drew her around to stand in front of him, facing the window.

He wrapped his arms around her waist and whispered against her ear, "What do you see?"

"The house?" she asked in confusion.

"Specifically, your window."

"Yes. So?" Then her brow cleared, and the heart that had been calming down from the fear began to race for an entirely different reason. "You've been watching me."

"You caught me red-handed." He chuckled. "Or should I say red-eyed? I'm a voyeur. I've watched you every night since you moved back upstairs. You undress in front of your closet, which is in my direct line of vision. You've never once closed your curtains."

She leaned back against his chest and felt his heart slamming against it. "I don't ever close them. We haven't had live-in servants since I was a little girl, and no one can see in my window."

"I can." He nipped her earlobe. "You don't know how many times I've wondered if that trellis will still hold my weight."

"All you have to do—" she curved an arm up and back to run her fingers through his hair "—is walk up the stairs."

With a feral growl, his arms tightened around her. "You're frustrating the hell out of me."

A sensuous, deeply satisfied smile curved her lips. "Good. It's nice to know I'm not alone."

He ran a line of kisses down her neck. "Witch."

She chuckled and turned in his arms. He was hard everyplace they touched—from the neck she'd wound her arms around, to the steely grip holding her, to the muscled planes of his chest, to the bulge pressing into her stomach. ''There's only one cure.''

''Then cure me. I can't stand it any longer.'' He lifted her to her toes and covered her mouth with his.

Heat shot through her, spiking into every corner of her body. His kiss was hungry, bruising, but she pushed herself closer still, relishing the strength of his passion.

When they touched, it was as if a broken circuit suddenly connected. The halves that were dead alone sprang to life, with an energy flowing between them as strong as the sun's.

His tongue probed, and she opened without hesitation. Her tongue joined his in the dance so closely imitating what they really craved. She moaned when his hands molded to the curves of her breasts. She arched against him, begging for more.

With a curse, he yanked her T-shirt over her head. The cool air bathed her, but the goose bumps rippling across her skin were from the heat within, not the air-conditioning. Her bra quickly followed, and her nipples puckered in anticipation. It had been so long since she'd felt the heat of a man's hand, the wet fire of his mouth. Way, way too long.

''Damn.'' His breath was a rough whisper. ''You're more beautiful than you were six years ago. How is that possible?''

His hands traveled up her sides to gently cup her breasts. She moaned as skin met skin. Rafe echoed the sound.

''You feel so good,'' he whispered. ''So incredibly soft and warm. And you taste—'' he bent her back over his arm, and his mouth replaced his hands ''—like the best aged whisky. Smooth and musky, but fiery going down.''

Flames blazed from his touch, making Emma's knees buckle, but she was held by the strong arm circling her hips.

''You like this, don't you?'' His teeth gently pulled at her nipple. ''I remember. God, I remember everything. This—'' his tongue traced a blazing path up to her neck, where it probed the hollows of her ear ''—drives you wild.''

Wild enough to want all of him. Now. She wanted to feel his

skin against hers. She wanted to rake her fingernails across his chest. She wanted to do to him what he was doing to her.

Grabbing the tail of his long-sleeved shirt, she yanked it from his jeans, then reached for his collar. She had no intention of wasting time with buttons. Buttons took too damn long.

She grasped the sides of his shirt and yanked it open. Buttons hit her naked flesh as they flew off. With a satisfied growl, she placed her hands on his chest, only to grab handfuls of undershirt.

"You're wearing too many clothes." Finding the hem of the T-shirt, she worked her hands underneath.

Encountering rough, ridged skin, she hesitated. "What's this?"

Suddenly her hands were seized in a steely grip, separating them.

Rafe released a torrent of curses, in both Spanish and English. His body was taut, his face anguished. "I can't do this."

If Emma could've, she would've slapped herself. "I know you're scarred, Rafe. I forgot for a second. I'm sorry."

He released her hands, then walked around the chair, away from her. "Maybe you should go."

"And maybe I shouldn't." She followed, shivering at the abrupt loss of his heat. "It doesn't matter, Rafe. Your scars don't make a damn bit of difference to me."

He turned to face her, then uttered a strangled sound as his gaze fell to her naked breasts, which she made no attempt to hide.

He tore his gaze away. "You haven't seen them."

She reached to touch the scar on his face. A fist of iron stopped her. "Please, Rafe. Give me another chance."

"Isn't what we have enough?" His hand squeezed her wrist so tightly she winced, and he released her. "We work together every day. We share a home, a family, an exciting new venture. Why do we have to share a bed?"

"Because you want me as much as I want you." She faced him squarely. "You've already admitted it."

Rafe plowed both hands back through his hair so hard she thought he'd tear every strand from his head. "I...just...can't."

"Why?"

He stared at her so long she thought he wouldn't answer. Finally he said softly, "Because I don't want to lose you. I don't want to lose the life I've found."

Her heart melted like chocolate under the hot Memphis sun. "You think I'm going to run away from a few scars?"

"You wouldn't be first. Even my mother cried every time she saw them. There's a hell of a lot more than a few."

She wanted to howl at him, to pound on his chest, to demand to know how he could work her libido up to a frenzy, then deny her. But he'd already been hurt so much, she couldn't hurt him anymore.

If she hadn't already known she loved him, she'd know it now.

"It sounds like I'm not the only one who doesn't know how to trust," she told him.

"Emma, I—"

"It's all right, *querido*. Of all people, I understand." She took his hand in hers and rubbed the scar on the back of his hand against her cheek. "But I'm warning you, I'm not giving up. You should remember by now that I'm a very stubborn woman. I loved you despite my father's wishes, and I didn't desert you until I thought you were dead. I'm not going to desert you now. Somehow I'm going to convince you to trust me."

He turned his hand to caress her cheek, his expression one of awe mixed with misery. "How could I ever have been enough man to deserve a woman like you?"

"You were an angel, Rafe. You're still my angel. I just didn't know how badly your wings had been broken." She smiled, despite the tears brimming in her eyes. "I guess now I have to take a crash course on setting angel wings."

Chapter Nine

"You got the Coca-Cola endorsement?" his mother said through the phone. "Oh, Rafe, that's wonderful! Oops. I mean, David."

Rafe smiled ruefully at the disdainful note in his mother's voice. She'd made no secret of the fact she disapproved of his name change. "It's okay, Mom. Call me Rafe."

"Is that the name you'll use in your magazine?"

"No. Sorry. I already have a reputation as David, so I'll stick to that for professional purposes." He glanced up as Emma opened the door to his apartment. "But to my family, I'm Rafe."

Emma hesitated when she saw him on the phone. He waved her in.

"I wish your father were here," his mother said, her voice fading. He could just see her peering out the kitchen window, up the driveway. "He should be home any min— Oh, good. There he is now. Hold on. I'll hurry him in."

The phone clunked as his mother laid it on the kitchen counter. Rafe smiled at Emma, who'd turned on the computer. "Finish cleaning up the kitchen?"

Emma returned his smile crookedly. "Finally. Lasagna is good, but Momma sure does make a mess when she cooks it."

He shifted the phone from one ear to the other. "I offered to help."

"I know." She sighed heavily. "But it's easier to just go ahead and do it myself than to listen to Momma argue until you leave."

He chuckled. "Is Gabe home yet?"

She shook her head as she sat down in front of the computer. "He's going to spend the night at Randy's. There's a Braves game on cable. He won't be home till morning."

Rafe nodded, then stood and stretched. Blessing whoever invented the cordless phone, he walked over and bent to give Emma a kiss.

With the breathless sigh he'd come to love, she leaned into him. She smiled languidly as he reluctantly straightened. Then, noticing what he held, she frowned. "Are you still on the phone?"

"Yep."

"On hold, I take it? Who are you talking to?"

He could hear the distant sound of his mother speaking excitedly to his father in Spanish. "My parents."

Emma went still. "Have you told them about us?"

"If I did, they'd be on the next plane to Memphis to meet their daughter-in-law and grandson. And since you haven't told Gabe he has another set of grandparents..."

With a wince, she looked away.

Rafe felt guilty reminding her of her trust issues when he had his own problems in that area. He placed a hand on her shoulder and bent to place a quick kiss on her forehead. "I'm sor—"

"David?" his father barked into the phone. "You still there?"

Rafe straightened and heard his mother haughtily inform her husband that he preferred to be called Rafe. "Yes, Dad. I'm—"

His father lifted him onto his shoulders. Rafe's heart pounded at the height, but his father's strong hands held him securely.

"Rafe?"

He shook his head, his heart pounding for real. A memory from his childhood. How...?

Then he realized he still had his hand on Emma's shoulder.

"Bandito! Come here!" Rafe slapped his legs, urging a brown mutt with a white mask to leave his mother's feet.

"Rafe?" His father's voice was louder this time.

"I'm here, Dad." Rafe pulled his hand from Emma's shoulder so he could concentrate on talking.

"You all right, son?"

"I'm fine. I just...got distracted for a second. Sorry."

"Your mother's been chattering on about you getting the Coca-Cola account."

Rafe spoke with his parents for another ten minutes, telling them about all he'd accomplished in the past week. As always, they were excited about his success and supportive of his plans.

Emma worked at the computer as he talked. She seemed to relax as the minutes passed. Rafe wanted to touch her again, to see if the two snatches of childhood had been a fluke. But they were so distracting, and he needed to concentrate on what he was saying or his parents would worry.

As he was about to hang up, however, he couldn't resist. He again placed his hand on Emma's shoulder.

He heard his mother shriek, "¡Ay, Dios mío!"

Rafe and Mike stopped pounding each other. Rafe glanced at her. She held her hands against her cheeks. Her mouth was open, her eyes wide.

Suddenly an uppercut clipped him on the jaw.

Mike had sneaked in a hit.

It wasn't a fluke. Just as she'd been the key to regaining memories of her, Emma could give him back his past. All of it.

"What? Oh. Goodbye... I love you, too... Yes. I'll come when I can. Goodbye."

He hit the talk button on the phone and set it on the nearest surface. He grabbed Emma's chair and spun her around to face him.

"Gracious!"

"Guess what?" he asked excitedly.

She grabbed his shoulders for balance. "What?"

His grin felt as if it was splitting his face. When he first began recalling his past, he thought he would retrieve it all, but he'd been disappointed. It seemed as if Emma could only give him the memories that concerned her. Now he knew he'd soon have his entire life back inside his head. He'd be whole again. Mentally, at least. "I just had some memories from when I was a kid."

She froze except for her green eyes widening. "What?"

"I touched you when I was on the phone to my parents and *poof!* There they came. I remembered one time when my father put me on his shoulders and a dog we used to have and a fight I had with my brother."

"Oh." She seemed stunned. "How...nice."

"Nice? It's great! Stupendous. Miraculous."

"Okay, I get the picture. Calm down, Mr. Thesaurus." Her frown deepened. "Are you sure they were memories?"

"They have to be. They were just snippets, really. Not as full as the ones I get with you. But maybe that's because it was over the phone. Maybe in person, they'd be longer, clearer." He grabbed her hands in his. "Don't you see what this means? If it's really true, it means I'll be whole again. I'll be Rafe again."

She sucked in a quick breath, then pulled a hand from his and laid it on his cheek. "I don't care about the old Rafe. I like this one. I want you just the way you are now."

His face softened, and he leaned down to kiss her forehead. "You make me feel like I'm twelve feet tall."

"You don't have to be twelve feet tall. The six feet you have is plenty. You're enough, Rafe. Just the way you are."

Her face was so earnest, so pleading, so intensely focused on him.

In a blinding flash, Rafe knew he loved her, had always loved her, even when he hadn't known she existed. She was the other half of not just his soul, but his entire being. That's why touching her made his memories return. She completed him.

Kneeling, he drew her into his arms. "Emma. *Mi vida.*"

My life. That's what she was.

She kissed him as if she wanted to brand herself on his soul. As if she wanted to burn every other thought from his mind.

She nearly succeeded. He pulled his lips from hers only when he was ready to pick her up and carry her into the bedroom.

As they caught their breath, he drew back to look at her. It was getting harder every day to deny her—and himself. He wanted her more than he wanted to see tomorrow. But if he gave in, there might not be any tomorrows with her.

"What am I enough for, Emma?" he asked, needing to remind her of her distrust, to justify his own.

She pressed her lips together, but didn't look away. Her gaze delved deep into his own, as if searching his soul. Finally, she said, "To keep around."

Surprise shot through him. This wasn't how the script had been reading. "What do you mean?"

"I mean—" She ran a hand gently down the scar on his cheek "—I'm ready to tell Gabe you're his father."

"What?" His surprise twisted into relief mixed with panic.

"If you like, we can walk down to Randy's now and get him. I'm sure he won't be disappointed to miss the Braves game once he finds out what we want to tell him."

Rafe brushed a strand of blond hair from her cheek. "Are you sure? Are you doing this because you want me or because you trust me?"

"Both," she whispered. "And also because of Gabe. He loves you, and he needs to know his father. I've been wrong to keep the news from him."

"You're not afraid I'm going to hurt you like I did before? Or like your father or Jerry?"

Her brow wrinkled. "Maybe a little. But like you said, you can't prove you won't hurt me. Only time can do that. I believe you don't want to. That's enough for now."

Rafe was both awed by her confidence and frightened by its implications. She'd proven she could overcome her misgivings. Now she would expect him to do the same.

"Do you want to go get Gabe?" she asked.

He shook his head. "Let him watch his game. Tomorrow will be soon enough to tell him."

She smiled sadly and bent to give him a solemn kiss. "All right, *querido*."

Her obvious disappointment brought his height from twelve feet to two inches.

He was so close to trusting her. He wanted to trust her. But he couldn't forget his niece's screams when she saw his scars, or the way his mother cried every time she helped him change his bandages. They both loved him, and look at the way they'd reacted.

No, he couldn't give in now. A day or two more was all he asked. Time to prepare himself for the revulsion he'd see on the beautiful face he loved so much. Time to prepare arguments why she shouldn't leave him.

"We'll tell him tomorrow," he told her. "Together."

"Okay." She gave him another kiss, then drew away and turned to the computer.

The next evening Emma pulled into the driveway at seven-fifteen. A last-minute, had-to-be-out project had come up at work, and she'd had to stay late.

Rafe's truck was not parked in its usual spot at the curb. Not that she'd expected it to be. This was Tuesday night, the last practice of the season for the T-Ball Tigers. She'd talked to Rafe that afternoon and told him to go ahead and take Gabe and Randy to practice. She'd make it if she could.

Which, of course, she couldn't. Practice would be over in fifteen minutes. So she gathered her things and got out of the car.

She'd been worrying all day about what she had to tell Gabe tonight. Despite her claim to trust Rafe, she was more than a little concerned, especially since he recalled memories from his childhood yesterday. What if he got them all back? Would he still want his son and wife, or would he leave them behind to return to the newspaper? And what would happen to *Southern Yesteryears?*

All she could do was trust him. All she had to do was put her welfare, her happiness, her life—and that of her son—into the hands of another man. The very thought terrified her.

In the kitchen Emma found a note from her mother. Sylvia was attending a meeting of her garden club and would be home around eight-thirty. She'd left a plate for Emma in the refrigerator.

Realizing Rafe and the boys would be home by the time she finished eating zapped her appetite, and she grabbed a soft drink instead. She downed it as she changed into shorts and a T-shirt so she could catch up on the dusting she hadn't had time to do in the past few weeks.

To keep herself from worrying, she thought about different ways to lay out the spread on the Hunt-Phelan House. Before she knew it, a car pulled into the driveway. She realized with surprise that it was nearly dark and glanced out the window to see her mother's old Cadillac pull into the garage.

Was it eight-thirty already? She looked at her watch to verify it. Eight twenty-six. Where were Rafe and the boys? They should've been home an hour ago.

Striding down the hall, she threw open the back door as her mother made her way down the walk. "Rafe isn't home with Gabe and Randy."

Sylvia shrugged as if unconcerned. "He just has Gabe. Randy's father picked him up around three."

"So where're Rafe and Gabe?"

"Rafe told me he's taking the team out for ice cream after practice, since it's the last one."

"What? Did he say where?"

Sylvia climbed the steps and opened the door to the screened porch. "No. I don't believe he told me that."

"Did he say when he'd be home?"

Her mother shook her head as she stepped onto the porch. "I expect it'll take an hour or so. Is something wrong?"

"We were supposed to tell Gabe tonight about Rafe being his father. But he's always so exhausted after practice he falls asleep right after his bath. Tonight we'll be lucky if he doesn't fall asleep in the tub."

Now Emma was really worried. Would Rafe take the opportunity to tell Gabe he was his father? He'd said they would tell him together. Would he remember that when he had his son all to himself for the first time?

She headed for the front door and began pacing the hallway. Darkness had fallen beyond the glass security door when she finally saw Rafe's truck pull up in front. It was after nine.

She pushed the screen door open and stepped onto the porch.

Rafe knew he was in trouble the minute he climbed out of the truck and saw Emma standing on the porch with her arms crossed over her stomach. Wondering what he'd done now, he walked around the cab to haul his sleeping son from the front seat.

He hadn't unbuckled the seat belt before Emma was at his side.

"What's wrong with him?"

Rafe released the catch, then turned to glare at her. "Nothing. He fell asleep on the way home."

She relaxed somewhat. "Oh."

Rafe reached for Gabe. "I am capable of taking my son out for an evening without hurting him."

"Where have you been? It's after nine."

"Parry Jenkins and I took the kids out for ice cream after practice. I told Sylvia. Didn't you get the message?"

Emma closed the truck door and followed him up the walk to the house. "Not until she came in at eight-thirty. Why didn't you leave me a note telling me where you were taking the kids so I could join you?"

He waited for her to open the security door for him. "You mean so you could protect your son from his father?"

Emma cast a frantic glance at Gabe. "Hush! He'll hear you. I don't want him to find out like this."

Rafe jiggled his son, who slept on. "He's oblivious. A meteor could crash in the street, and he'd never wake up. Now, are we going to stand here and argue, or can I take him to bed?"

She finally opened the door. "What about his bath?"

"He can sleep dirty tonight," Rafe said.

"But—"

"Everything all right?" Sylvia asked from the living room.

"We're fine, Momma," Emma answered. "You watching your soaps?"

"I just popped the first one in, but if you need me, I can—"

"That's all right, Sylvia." Rafe headed up the stairs. "We're fine."

Emma followed. She fussed over Gabe, brushing his hair from his face, tsking over the dirt as she undressed him. When she started toward the bathroom for a wet cloth, Rafe steered her toward the stairs instead.

"He's dirty," she protested. "I need to—"

"Let him sleep," Rafe said. "You can wash the dirt off tomorrow."

She raised a brow. "Fine. That gives us a chance for a little talk."

Rafe rolled his eyes and started down the stairs. "I don't need this right now, Emma. I looked at office locations all morning, fought with the computer all afternoon, then ran around the field tonight because you weren't there to do it for me. My leg hurts like hell, and the only thing I want to do is fill that claw-foot bathtub in my apartment with hot water and soak for three days.''

"We need to talk.''

"In the morning.''

"I have to go to work in the morning.''

He sighed heavily. "Fine. But you'll have to talk through the bathroom door. I can't wait to get out of these sweaty clothes.'' At the bottom of the stairs, he turned toward the back door. "Good night, Sylvia.''

"Good night, Rafe,'' she called. "Pleasant dreams.''

"You wouldn't get so sweaty if you'd wear shorts and a T-shirt like a normal person,'' Emma told him.

He glared as he held the back door open for her. "Very funny.''

"You're the only one who cares about your scars, Rafe. I don't. And the kids sure don't.''

He paused on the walk. "I'm not in the mood for this conversation, Emma. If this is what you want to talk about, you might as well turn right back around and go to bed.''

"It's not.''

"Fine.'' He swept his arm toward the garage. "After you.''

He frowned at her bottom as they walked up the stairs, amazed that his body could still react when he was tired, aching and cranky. He unlocked the apartment, then followed her in.

"Did you tell Gabe?'' she asked in an accusing voice as soon as he'd closed the door.

"Did I tell Gabe what?'' he returned.

"About you being his father.''

Leaning back against the door, Rafe closed his eyes and groaned. "Is that what this is about?''

"Did you?''

He straightened and gave her another glare. "No. But not because I didn't want to.'' He stomped into the bathroom and closed the door with a satisfying click.

She opened it. "We can't talk through the door.''

"I thought we were finished."

She crossed her arms over her stomach. "What did you two talk about in the truck?"

He pushed her out of the doorway. "I'll leave the door open a few inches so you can yell at me."

"I'm not yelling."

"Whatever." He pulled the door, but left a six-inch gap. Then he turned on the water, adjusting the flow until a satisfying steam rose from the tub.

"What did you and Gabe talk about?" Emma called over the din.

"What do you think? Baseball." Glancing at the door to be certain he wasn't in Emma's line of sight, he unbuttoned his shirt. "He told me about the Braves game on TV last night. Then we talked about the different positions on the T-ball team."

"That's it?"

He yanked his shirt off and pulled his undershirt over his head. "It only takes twenty minutes to get to the park. Did you expect us to come up with a plan for world peace?"

"I just— It's the first time you and Gabe have been alone together for any length of time."

He twisted off his watch. "Yeah. I noticed."

"We were planning to tell him tonight," she retorted. "I thought you might have decided to go ahead, seeing as it was so late."

He peeled off his socks and shoes. "I didn't."

"Why not?"

"Did you want me to?" He'd never met a more stubborn woman in all his life. "I didn't tell him because—silly me—I thought you were beginning to trust me, and I didn't want to do anything to jeopardize that. I thought we were planning to tell him together."

He turned on the water in the sink to brush his teeth. The added noise drowned out her reply. "What?"

''I said we were.'' He could tell she'd leaned closer to the opening in the door.

He squirted toothpaste onto his brush. ''Then what's your problem?''

Again, her answer was lost. Shrugging, Rafe popped the toothbrush into his mouth. He spent the recommended two minutes brushing his teeth, then bent over the sink to rinse. Straightening, he dropped the toothbrush into a slot in the ceramic holder, then caught a movement in the steamy mirror.

Whirling abruptly, he froze, but inside his heart plummeted, bouncing hard as it hit the soles of his feet.

Emma had pulled the door open. She stood swathed in steam, staring at his chest. Tears streamed down her face.

Chapter Ten

Emma stared without blinking at Rafe's rough, battered body. The scars she'd pictured had been nothing like this. Puckered pink skin, evidence of second- and third-degree burns, reached diagonally down from his left shoulder to disappear into his jeans at his hip. Layered on top of that and scattered all over his chest, neck and arms, were so many ugly jagged slashes she couldn't count them all. Among them were the clean, precise cuts of surgical scars.

"Oh, my God, Rafe." Her husky whisper sounded dead in the thickly humid air. "No wonder you forgot everything. It's a miracle you survived at all."

He stood rigid, his face tight. "Get out."

His words brought her head up. "What?"

"You've seen the freak show. Now leave."

Her eyes narrowed as the past faded away. If he thought he could get rid of her, he had about fifty more thinks coming. "So this is it? This is what you've been so careful to hide from me all this time?"

"I told you it wasn't a pretty sight."

"You're right. It isn't."

He turned away from her to grasp the sink with a white-knuckled grip. If anything, his back was worse than his chest. "Just get out."

Anger wrapped around Emma like the steamy swirls of his bath. Anger that he thought she would run screaming from the sight. Anger that he hadn't remembered her for six and a half years. Anger that she hadn't been there to help him through the pain. Anger for all the time they'd lost.

She knew part of her anger was irrational. He couldn't help not remembering her. But being irrational just made her angrier.

"The hell I will."

"Emma..."

"How dare you!"

He turned as she took a step toward him, her hands clenched into fists at her sides. "Emma, you don't—"

"You've been making me feel guilty for weeks—weeks!—thinking my lack of trust was the reason we couldn't settle our differences. But *you've* been worse than I ever *thought* about being. At least I had Gabe to think about. All you had was your stupid vanity."

"That's not fair," he growled.

She threw her arms in the air. "You want to talk about fair? Was it fair of you to assume I'd run screaming at the sight of a few little scars?"

"Few? Little?"

She poked him repeatedly on his one good shoulder. "God forbid you be the one to take a risk. You insisted I be the one to crack first. But even when I did, you refused to have anything to do with me. What the hell do you think that's done for *my* vanity? Huh, buster?"

He grabbed her hand to stop her from poking him. "Take a good, long look at me, Emma. Can you honestly say you don't find me repulsive?"

"Yes," she said without hesitation.

He searched her face belligerently, as if looking for an excuse not to believe her. "How?"

She took a deep breath. So she had to be the first one to take this risk, too. Then she realized she wanted to. Even if he didn't return her feelings, she wanted him to know how she felt. "Because I love you."

Rafe went still. "You love me?"

She took advantage of his shock to wrap her arms around him. "Of course I love you, you idiot." She ran her hand over the rough skin of his shoulder. "I love every scar..."

"Emma, don't..."

She bent to kiss a glossy crevice on his neck. "Every burned inch..."

"Please..."

Her next kiss followed a sliding path across the jagged, foot-long gash that slashed across his chest. "Every ridge and bump and muscle."

Rafe pulled her close and buried his face in her hair. "You don't mean it. You can't."

She jerked back and glared at him. "You say something stupid like that again and I guess I'll just have to beat it into your brain. I should know if I love you or not, so don't you dare go telling me what I do and don't mean."

Her angry words washed over Rafe like a healing rain. The words found their way into every dark corner of his being. He felt as strong and whole and light as the angel she'd drawn him as so many years ago.

"How could you love someone like me?" he asked.

Her face softened. "Sometimes I wonder that myself. If God had to send me an angel to love, why did it have to be one with broken wings?"

Rafe frowned. "I never was an angel."

"You were to me. Your wings weren't really broken when we loved each other six years ago. I loved you then because you were handsome and cocky and strong." She ran her hands down his arms. "Your wings are broken now, but that doesn't make you less of a man. In fact, you're twice the man you were when I married you. Now you're patient instead of reckless. You're confident instead of cocky. As well as handsome and strong."

He shook his head. "Not handsome."

She placed a hand on either side of his face. "To me, you're beautiful. But people don't love angels because they're beautiful. They love them because they're sent from God. Their beauty comes from within. I love you for what's inside of you, Rafe. For the part of you that can never be burned away. These scars have made you what you are, and because of that, I love them, too."

He searched her face for any hint of hesitation, but all he could see was love. How could he not believe?

Tears burning the back of his eyes, he folded his arms around her and held her close. He'd finally found someone who not only accepted him—she loved every part of him. She saw his scars not as the ordeal he'd gone through, but as the journey he'd traveled.

"You're my wife and I'm never going to let you go," he whispered.

She placed her lips against his neck. "You'd better not. Or you'll be a fallen angel as well as one with broken wings because I'll make your life a living hell."

He drew back enough to smile down into her beautiful face. "Emma. *Mi vida. Mi corazón. Mi esposa.*"

She smiled crookedly. "What? Not going to say your heart needs an EKG?"

He chuckled. "I really did use such an awful pun, didn't I?"

"Among others. You—"

She broke off as water came spilling over the edge of the tub.

Cursing, Rafe plunged his hand into the water to yank on the stopper while Emma turned off the faucet. She grabbed the towels off the shelf and threw them on the puddle. He bent to wipe up the water, then tossed the towels on the hamper.

He turned to find her smiling at him. His body flared with desire, but the water reminded him of what he'd been about to do. "I need to take a bath. I'm all sweaty."

"Then let's kill two birds with one stone." She smiled sultrily. "I've always wondered if this old tub is big enough for two.

Love for this beautiful woman filled him until his skin felt tight, until he felt as if it overflowed the boundaries of his body like the water had overflowed the tub. Stepping close, he ran a finger down her soft, smooth cheek. "It does, you know."

Her arms circled his waist as if they knew their way. "You've tried it, have you? With who?"

"I'm talking about my heart, not the tub. It needs you." He placed a kiss on her lips. "I need you."

"I've been trying to tell you that for a week," she complained.

Reminded of how she'd been trying to seduce him, he groaned. "Damn it. We can't do anything tonight. You said I'm confident, but I haven't been confident enough to buy protection."

"Stupid man." She gave him an irritated shake. "You should always be prepared."

He tried to keep his frustration from showing as he slid his hands down the curve of her back. He kissed her temple in apology, knowing if he touched her lips he wouldn't give a damn about protection. "I'm sorry. More sorry than you could ever know. It's just that I believed I'd never need protection again, though I hoped against hope for a miracle—like this one."

"I should let you suffer tonight like I've been suffering for a week. It would be your just reward for not believing in me."

"You're right." He lifted his brows hopefully. "But what do you mean, *should* let me suffer?"

She smiled like a cat that had cornered a mouse. "I mean, faithless man, that *I'm* prepared." Taking his hand, she led him into the office where she opened the drawer in the computer desk and pulled out a box of condoms. "See?"

Desire and relief swept through him as he took the box from her hand. Thank God they didn't have to wait.

He glanced at the box, then at her, his brow rising. "Only six?"

She laughed out loud—a joyful, playful laugh—and stepped into his waiting arms. "If we run out, there's a twenty-four hour drugstore at the corner of Union and McLean."

Chuckling, he bent, caught her behind the knees and lifted her. "The way I feel, I'll be making a run around midnight."

"Sounds like I've unleashed a monster." She laced her hands behind his neck. "Finally."

He shook his head. "Just an angel who wants to see if this earthly pleasure is as good as his memories."

"Oh, it is," she said, her voice husky. "But you let me know, you hear? We'll keep trying until we get it right."

He strode into the bathroom, determined to hold her to her promise.

Emma woke to the sound of a door opening. Groggy, she turned over and grimaced as sunshine hit her full in the face. With a loud squeak, the door closed. That and the tired soreness of her body reminded her where she was and what she'd been doing.

She smiled.

"Dreaming of me, I hope."

She opened her eyes to see Rafe standing over her, carrying a tray. She caught a glimpse of her mother's best silver. "What's this?"

"Breakfast." He laid the tray on the dresser, then knelt one knee on the bed.

She sat up, pushing hair from her face. "I don't suppose you fixed it."

He claimed a kiss, then gave her a rueful smile as he sat on the bed. "You think Sylvia would let me?"

Emma groaned. "I suppose it would've been too much to ask to keep our sex life to ourselves for a few days."

"Especially when you sleep so late."

Her gaze cut to the clock. "What time is it? Nine-fifteen?" She threw her leg over the side of the bed. "I'm late for work."

He caught her arm, preventing her from rising. "Relax. Sylvia called in sick for you."

"She did?" Emma turned to see his eyes traveling down her naked body bared when the sheet had slipped. She smiled at the desire raging across his face. After a night of lovemaking, he still hadn't gotten enough. Good. Neither had she. "Rafe?"

"Hmm?"

"We can't make love. We used all the condoms."

He blinked, as if bringing his mind back from a faraway place. "We did? All six?"

She smiled wryly. "Counting the one I put my nail through because I was in such a hurry."

"Damn. I really was as randy as a teenager." He slipped an arm around her waist and pulled her onto his lap.

Emma's chuckle broke apart as he swept his hand up her stomach to caress her breast. She enjoyed the rough heat of his palm and the dark blaze in his eyes for a long moment. Then with a moan, she turned over and bit his jean-clad thigh close to his hip. "That's for making me want you when we can't do anything about it."

He stood abruptly, digging into his pocket for his keys. "Where was that drugstore again?"

He strode to the door, then stopped suddenly and released a torrent of Spanish curses.

"What's wrong?" she asked.

He faced her. "Gabe and Randy will see me going to the truck, and they'll want to go. How would I explain what I'm buying? Blow one up and tell them they're balloons?"

"Gabe's home?" Emma sat and pulled the sheet up over her body. "Of course he is. Randy's always here by seven-thirty. How did— What did Gabe say about me being up here?"

"I had to think of something fast, and I wanted it to be something they'd understand." Rafe's eyes danced with laughter. "So I told them we had a sleepover just like they did."

Emma couldn't suppress a giggle. "A sleepover?"

He nodded. "Gabe wanted to come up and see you, but I told him you were still sleeping because—" he chuckled "—because we stayed up late having pillow fights. I thought Sylvia was going to choke."

Laughing, Emma fell back on the pillows. Seconds later, the bed dipped as Rafe knelt over her. She reached a hand up to caress his handsome face. "I enjoyed our 'pillow fights.'"

"Me, too." He grinned widely and bent to kiss her. "And I plan on having a helluva lot more."

"You do?"

He searched her eyes, then stretched out beside her. His face thoughtful, he took her hand in his. "Will you marry me, Emma?"

She smiled and laced her fingers with his. "We're already married."

"Do you want to stay married? Act married? Live like we're married?"

She answered with no hesitation. "Yes."

Relief smoothed the lines between his brows. "So how are we going to explain our suddenly moving in together to everyone? How are you going to explain that Gabe's name has been Johnson all along, never Lockwood? How are you going to explain that you married another man when you were still married to me?"

"I thought you were dead."

"You didn't have my death certificate. How did you marry Lockwood so quickly?"

Her gaze fell. "My father made me lie when they asked me if I'd been married before. I still can't believe I knuckled under so easily. I was so young, and I felt lost because you were gone."

"Wouldn't it be better if you didn't have to explain that to everyone? It's none of their business. I don't want to put you through that."

He was protecting her. But not in a macho, take-charge kind of way. He was giving her a choice. Emma's heart expanded with so much love, it felt as if it was reaching out to touch his. This was proof of what he'd told her at the beginning—that he didn't want to run her life, just share it. This was why she loved him more now than ever.

She turned on her side to fully face him. "A wedding would cut down on explanations."

He rested his hand on her hip. "A ceremony will also make it seem that much more real to us. We've been apart for so long. And it will give our families the chance to hear us repeat our vows. We'll tell Gabe, of course, and my family."

"I don't want a big, elaborate wedding."

"No, there's no need for that. Something quiet, maybe here at home."

Emma ran her hands across his broad shoulders, already intimately familiar with the warm, rough texture. She loved the way he thought of this as his home.

He kissed her forehead softly. "I *would* like to get the father's name changed on Gabe's birth certificate. I'll have to find out what we have to do, but I'll make sure it's done quietly. I don't even know if it's possible. It should be, with all the paternity suits in the courts."

At that moment she realized how much Rafe was willing to give up to protect her. "But everyone will think you've just adopted Gabe. They won't know he's your biological son."

He shrugged. "People won't think less of me for adopting your son, so that doesn't matter. What counts is that it will be there in black and white for Gabe, and for future generations, to know for sure."

"Oh, Rafe." She wrapped her arms around his neck and pulled him close. "I love you so much."

"I love you, too, *querida.*"

She drew back. "You do?"

He smoothed strands of hair from her face. "Of course I do. What the hell do you think I've been telling you for the past twelve hours?"

"You never said the words," she pointed out.

"I didn't?" He placed an apologetic kiss on her lips. "I'm sorry. In my mind, it was absolutely, positively clear."

Relief washed away her doubts, like a wave clearing the beach.

He ducked from under her arms. "Stay right there. I have something I want to give you."

She rose to her elbow and watched as he fished around in a dresser drawer. "What?"

"Can't guess?" A moment later he sat on the bed facing her, grinning like a little boy who'd made his mother a Valentine. He took her left hand and slipped a ring on her finger. "Your wedding ring."

Emma's smile faded as the heavy stone of the University of Texas class ring slid around to the underbelly of her finger. The doubts that had been recently washed away came seeping back. This was the ring he'd given her when she was nineteen.

She looked up into his beaming face. Who did he love? Emma the woman or Emma the girl?

"What's wrong?" he asked.

"It's..." She flicked the stone back into place, only to have it slide around the other side. "It's so big."

"I thought since—" Frowning, he reached to take it back.

Emma closed her fist to prevent him. "I never actually wore it on my finger, except for our wedding night. I'll just have to get used to it."

He shook his head. "I'll buy you a real one. Everyone will expect me to, anyway."

"I want to keep your ring, Rafe. It was part of me for so long."

"Okay." But his smile didn't quite reach his eyes.

The joy of the past night dimmed. His obvious hurt made her

suspect that when he looked at her, loved her, he saw the Emma in his memories, not the Emma in his bed.

To her, this ring symbolized their relationship six and a half years ago. She worried that he saw it the same way.

Maybe it was selfish of her, but she wanted a new ring, a fresh start, proof that he loved her for who she was now, not for who she was then.

"Your breakfast is getting cold." She rose from the bed. "I'll get dressed. Then we can decide how to tell Gabe."

"Yeah?" Sandwiched on the couch by his parents, Gabe looked expectantly first at Rafe, then his mother.

Rafe glanced at Emma. They'd ended up waiting until after supper to talk to Gabe, and that morning they'd agreed the news should come from Emma.

She gave him a nervous smile over their son's head, then bent her attention to Gabe. She took his hand in hers. "You know how you've always wondered why Jerry doesn't come see you?"

Gabe nodded. "Other divorced dads visit their kids."

Rafe wondered how many kids Gabe knew whose parents were divorced. Knowing the divorce rate, it was probably the norm rather than the exception. He vowed it would never happen to his son.

"Well, the reason why he never visits is—" Emma took a deep breath "—he isn't really your father."

Gabe leaned forward to peer into his mother's face. "He isn't?"

"No. You see, a long time ago I—"

"Is Rafe my dad?" Gabe turned his bright-eyed attention to him. "Rafe, are you my dad?"

Rafe glanced at Emma and received her nod of approval, then he laid his hand on Gabe's slender shoulder. "Yes, son, I am. I've been your father all along."

Gabe's face lit up like a Christmas tree. "I knew it!" He scrambled onto Rafe's lap to hug his neck.

Emotion choking him, Rafe wrapped his arms around the slender body, hugging his son so tight Gabe yelped. Loosening his hold, he met the dark eyes so like his own.

"I'm glad," Gabe said with the proud simplicity of a child.

"Me, too," Rafe said.

Emma scooted closer. "How did you know?"

Their son shrugged. "Everyone says how much I look like him. Then last week when I messed up, Gams told me to 'just wait until my dad got home.' When Rafe got home, him and me had this long 'cussion. So I was hoping maybe he was my dad."

Emma rolled her eyes. "Trust Momma to give it away."

"I wish she'd done it weeks ago," Rafe said.

Emma had the grace to look sheepish. She pushed back a lock of Gabe's hair. "I'm sorry I didn't tell you sooner, Gabe. I just—"

"That's okay, Mom." Gabe turned back to Rafe. "Does this mean I can call you Dad?"

Rafe ruffled the hair Emma had just straightened. "You'd better."

Gabe cocked his head to the side. "Are we divorced?"

Rafe met Emma's eyes. They'd decided it would be better not to go into the full story with Gabe. He was too young to understand everything that had led them to this point. They'd tell him when he was older.

But they didn't want to lie to him, either.

Emma avoided it by not answering his question directly. "Rafe and I are going to get married in a couple of weeks. Then your last name and mine will be Johnson, not Lockwood."

"You'll never have to worry about us getting divorced, son. Because we never will." Rafe leaned over and kissed his wife, sealing the vow.

Gabe covered his eyes. "Eeewww! Mushy stuff!"

Laughing, Rafe bent his son back and tickled his stomach. "Get used to it. You're going to be seeing a whole lot more mushy stuff from now on." He pulled Gabe upright and placed a kiss on his cheek. "I love your mother very much, and I love you, too."

With a beatific smile, Gabe slid one arm around Rafe's neck, then reached over to wrap the other around Emma's. "Now we're a real fam'ly."

Rafe and Emma added their own arms to the group hug, entwining each other and their son until Rafe couldn't tell where one ended and the others began.

He wished it could last forever.

Chapter Eleven

Emma slipped her hand into Rafe's as they walked out of the printer, located in an old refurbished warehouse along the bluffs south of downtown Memphis. The July air was thick with heat and humidity.

Rafe smiled down at her. "Well, for better or worse, our first baby has gone to bed."

Emma squeezed his hand. "Our second baby."

He bent and kissed her nose. "All right, our second. I keep forgetting, since I never saw Gabe as a baby."

"And whose fault is that?" she asked with an arched brow.

Rafe rolled his eyes. "You're never going to let me forget it, are you?"

"Nope."

"You're not playing fair. I had amnesia."

"Of course it's not fair." She grinned playfully. "That's what makes it so much fun."

"Impudent woman. Why, I ought to—"

"Ought to what?" She walked her fingers up his chest. She didn't have the slightest qualm that he would hurt her.

He backed her up against the hot truck and leaned into her. "I ought to kiss you silly."

She wound her arms around his neck. "Oh, yes, please do."

He grinned at her. "Flirt."

"Anything that works," she whispered, pulling his head down to hers.

He kissed her deeply, then drew away with a groan. "That's it. Get me all hot and bothered in the middle of a parking lot."

"Hey. You're not the one sizzling against the hot metal of this truck."

He kissed her again, briefly, then opened the passenger door. "Come on. I need to stop by the *Commercial Appeal.*"

Emma froze. "The *Commercial Appeal?* Why?"

"I'm placing a classified ad in Sunday's edition for a business manager. If we're going to put an issue out every month, I've got to have help. Are you sure you don't—"

"You already talked me into giving my notice at Harrison. I don't want you to spend more money than is absolutely necessary until we're sure the magazine is going to be successful." Relieved he wasn't planning on visiting his friend, Jay Patten, she climbed onto the truck's bench seat and let Rafe close the door. When he got in the other side, she continued, "Working full-time, I can handle the size it is now. We'll talk about hiring someone to help me with layout when we add pages."

"All right." Rafe started the engine and turned the air conditioner on full blast, then reached for Emma's hips and dragged her over.

"What are you—"

He covered her mouth with his.

Surprise was the only thing that made Emma hesitate an instant before she leaned into him with a sigh. She'd never get enough of kissing him, holding him. Not if they lived forever.

Finally, he drew away. "It's been five whole hours since we made love."

She shook her head in smiling disbelief. "We can't do it here."

"You started it." He pulled her tighter against him. "Besides, there's not much around here but some old warehouses."

Emma rewarded him for his passion with another kiss. "People come and go all the time. What would they think if they saw a truck bouncing up and down?"

He trailed kisses down her throat. "Who cares?"

She leaned her head back to give him better access. She was caring less and less by the minute. But when he nibbled gently through the layers of her blouse and bra, she pushed at his shoulders. "I thought you needed to go by the *Commercial Appeal*."

He raised his head, looking so adorably rumpled and heavy-lidded she almost pressed him back into her arms.

"You're right. Damn. What am I thinking?"

She combed her fingers through his hair. "I don't think you are. At least, not with your brain."

"My brain loves you every bit as much as...another part of my anatomy." He gave her a lopsided grin. "Which happens to be cussing my brain at the moment."

"We'd better go before your brain loses the argument." She gave him a quick kiss and tried to scoot across the seat.

Rafe's strong arms kept her in place. "Where are you going?"

"Back to my seat."

He reached for the middle seat belt. "Your place is next to me."

She let him buckle her in, then leaned against him, sliding her arm across his shoulders. "We look like a couple of teenagers."

"Who cares?" He leaned down to give her a kiss, then straightened and put the truck in gear.

He showed her several century-old warehouses that were being refurbished into offices. He'd looked at them for when *Southern Yesteryears* outgrew the rooms over the garage. He'd already told her he expected that to be around six months, soon after the space would be available.

It only took a few minutes to reach the *Commercial Appeal* on Union Avenue. The counter handling classified ads was in the lobby, so it wouldn't take long for Rafe to place the ad he'd already written. But the afternoon was so hot, Emma accompanied him inside.

She was glad she did because they had to wait in line. They hadn't been standing there five minutes, however, when a loud voice caught their attention.

"Rafe? Rafe Johnson, is that you?"

"Ham Gordon," Rafe said without hesitation. "Good to see you."

Emma wondered how Rafe remembered the editor Jay had been trying to talk Rafe into working for—until she realized Rafe was holding her hand.

She should've waited in the truck.

Mr. Gordon shook Rafe's other hand effusively. "It's about time you came to see me."

Rafe stared at the man a long second, then blinked hard. "Sorry I..." He shook his head as if clearing it. "I just came to place a classified."

Rafe turned to her, his eyes dazed. His voice sounded like it was on automatic pilot as he introduced her. "Emma, this is Ham Gordon. He and I worked together years ago. He's now the senior international editor here. Ham, this is my...fiancée, Emma Grey."

Suddenly Emma knew what was happening. Rafe was remembering the years he worked for the newspaper. She felt as if some giant fist had grabbed her heart to stop it from beating. Yanking her hand from Rafe's, she stepped away from him and offered it to Mr. Gordon. "Nice to meet you."

"Well, well. A pleasure to meet you, too. When's the happy event?"

"In two weeks," she said, casting nervous glances at Rafe.

Mr. Gordon rolled onto his heels and returned his attention to

Rafe. "So this is why you moved back to Memphis. You dog, you. Does Jay know? He didn't mention anything about it."

"He doesn't know yet," Emma said. "We're having a quiet ceremony with just the family."

Mr. Gordon nodded and swept his arm toward the carefully guarded entrance to the newspaper. "Would you like a tour? Rafe, I'm sure you'd like to see what's changed since you left."

"We need to—" Emma choked up when she saw the excited anticipation in her husband's eyes.

"I'd really like to see everything, if you've got time," Rafe said.

"I sure do!" The editor rubbed his hands together. "Let me take care of that classified. You got it all written out?"

Rafe reached into his shirt for a folded sheet of paper while Emma glared at him.

When Mr. Gordon stepped behind the counter to pull his rank, she quietly but firmly said, "We need to get home."

"Why?"

"Momma's going out with friends tonight."

"Not until after supper." Rafe's reply was distracted. He made no attempt to hide his excitement as he watched the editor go behind the counter to talk with the woman. He barely knew Emma was there. He certainly didn't know she was upset—so upset, she wanted to drag him out of the building before the editor returned.

But the man rejoined them before she could. "Ready?"

Rafe nodded without even looking at her. He captured her hand and followed Mr. Gordon. The editor checked them in at the security desk, where they were given badges to wear as they toured the building.

She had to give Mr. Gordon an *A* for strategy. He began the tour with advertising, then took them through typesetting and printing, ending up in editorial—the floor Rafe was most familiar with.

Rafe kept a tight grip on Emma's hand the whole time.

She watched him as they walked from place to place. She could almost see the synapses connecting in his brain, bringing him another link to his past. He remembered quite a few people, usually secretaries and union workers like film strippers and pressmen. Most of the reporters he'd known had moved on to other newspapers, but there were still a few left who knew him.

When Mr. Gordon took Rafe to his old desk, which sat against a wall in a room full of desks just like it, the look on her husband's face made Emma suck in a quick breath. She remembered what he'd said.

Investigative reporting requires an excellent memory. Something I don't have.

She pulled her hand from his, but she was too late. His memories had already surfaced.

Rafe ran his hands along the edge. "Whoever sits here now is a helluva lot neater than I ever was."

"Nobody has it now," the editor told him. "I'm looking for someone to fill the position you held, though. Interested?"

Rafe's face held such nostalgia and longing, Emma had to press her lips together to keep from crying out.

Finally Rafe shook his head, but it was with obvious reluctance. "I've got a magazine to run."

Was that just an excuse to avoiding telling Mr. Gordon about his amnesia? Or was he truly interested only in *Southern Yesteryears?*

"We need to get home." Emma hoped her voice didn't sound quite as choked to them as it did to her.

To her relief, Rafe nodded. Mr. Gordon showed them out, telling Rafe to come back and see him. Rafe gave him a noncommittal answer and walked her to the truck.

After she'd climbed into the seat, he leaned in and kissed her. "Thanks for being there."

"Did you—" She cleared her throat "remember much?"

"So much I felt overwhelmed."

Now that he had the memories from his reporting days, all that remained hidden from him were the ones from his childhood.

And his family would be here in two weeks for the wedding.

What the hell was she going to do?

She had to use these two weeks to bind him to her—with loving words, sweet kisses, hot sex, whatever worked—so that leaving her for any reason would be the last thing on his mind.

Rafe turned and looked longingly at the building. "I was a damn good reporter, and I had a lot of good times here."

She turned his face back to her. "You're a damn good editor, too. And we'll have a lot of good times launching *Southern Yesteryears.*"

He smiled and gave her another kiss. "Yes, we will."

But his heart wasn't in his words.

She hoped two weeks would be long enough.

When Emma came in from work the next evening, Rafe's truck wasn't in its usual spot. She entered the house, placed her things on the chest in the hall, then found her mother stirring creamed corn. She walked over and kissed her cheek. "Hi, Momma. Where are our menfolk?"

Sylvia smiled indulgently at her daughter. "The boys went over to Randy's to play on his computer. Audra got home early. I don't know where Rafe went, but he said he'd be home for supper."

Emma was struck by the easy way her mother said Rafe would be *home* for supper. Of course, Sylvia had been certain all along that Emma and Rafe would resume their marriage. When they'd told her about their plans for a small wedding, she'd approved wholeheartedly and insisted on helping plan it.

"Anything I can do to help supper along?" Emma asked.

Her mother shook her head. "All that needs doing is setting the table."

Emma took the hint and fished out the silverware. At ten of

six, Rafe's truck pulled up at the curb. Emma watched him climb out and head toward the house.

"Dad! Wait!" The call came faintly through the windows.

Rafe stopped and turned toward the Jenkins's house two doors down. Emma smiled at the grin on his face. He loved for Gabe to call him Dad.

Gabe scrambled up to sit on his father's shoulders. Smiling, Emma stepped into the hall to open the door.

"Hi, guys."

"Hi, Mom!"

Rafe kissed her. *"Te querida."*

She smiled. "I love you, too. Y'all get washed up, okay? Supper's about ready."

Rafe caught Gabe at the waist and flipped him to the floor. Gabe landed on his feet and took off for the bathroom.

Rafe took the opportunity to give her another kiss. "I've got a surprise for you." He patted his shirt pocket. "Damn. I must've left them in the truck."

Emma rolled her eyes. "What did you buy this time?"

"I—"

"Dad? You coming?"

He gave her another kiss. "I'll tell you later."

Emma watched his uneven steps take him to the bathroom, then went to help her mother dish up supper. When they sat down to eat, Gabe was well launched into a detailed explanation of the baseball computer game he and Randy had been playing. So Emma forgot about Rafe's surprise.

Rafe and Gabe pitched in to clear the table and clean the kitchen. The day after she and Rafe had rekindled their intimate relationship, Rafe told Emma that he didn't want his son to grow up thinking that a woman's place was in the kitchen. Their son's future was in the twenty-first century, not the nineteenth. He asked if it would be all right for him and Gabe to help with the kitchen chores from then on. He hadn't brought it up before, he said, because he didn't want to interfere with the way she was raising him. She was doing an excellent job, he insisted, but he really wanted to set a good example for his son.

How could Emma have argued with help cleaning the kitchen?

Sylvia pursed her lips the first couple of nights, of course, and Gabe had grumbled, but they soon realized Rafe meant what he said. Last night Rafe had insisted Sylvia take it easy while they did the work, and he did the same tonight.

Emma loved it, because it was that much more time she could spend with her husband and son. When they finished, Gabe took off to Randy's. As she and Rafe stood on the porch watching him run down the street to the Jenkinses', Emma finally remembered Rafe's promise.

"So what's this big surprise?" she asked.

He pulled her into his arms and kissed her.

She grinned. "That bad, huh?"

"I'm not trying to soften you up," he insisted. "I just wanted to kiss you."

"Uh-huh. C'mon. Out with it."

He smiled so proudly she thought he must've discovered a cure for the common cold. Then he said, "Tomorrow morning you, Gabe and I are flying to Houston."

Emma's heart careened wildly, then came to a screeching halt. "What?"

"Just a quick trip," he said, oblivious to her reaction. "We'll come back Sunday."

Feeling like the universe had suddenly collapsed, she stepped away and crossed her arms over her stomach. "Why?"

The question was more of a delaying tactic. She already knew the answer. He wanted to recover all his memories. The only ones missing were from his childhood.

This couldn't be happening. Not now. She'd planned a carefully laid web of loving seduction which she hoped would bind him to her with unbreakable bonds. All she needed was more time.

Her reaction must've finally penetrated his excitement because his smile faded into a perplexed frown. He placed his hands on her arms. "My parents want to meet you and Gabe."

She kept her arms crossed despite the gentle pressure he exerted to pull them away. "They'll be here in two weeks for the wedding."

"I know, but they—"

"You want to go so you can remember your childhood." Her tone was accusing, but she couldn't help it.

He searched her face. "What's wrong, *querida?*"

"I...tomorrow's Friday. I have to work. I still owe Harrison Printing another week on my notice."

"Surely one day won't—"

"No. I can't go."

His hands dropped away from her. "Why?"

"I told you—"

"Don't give me that 'I have to work' stuff. If Gabe were sick, you'd miss tomorrow."

She lifted her chin. "He isn't."

Rafe stared at her as if he'd never seen her before. "You won't go because I want memories from my childhood?"

Emma's heart hung in her throat like a lead balloon. The way he put it made it sounded so callous, so uncaring. But it wasn't that way at all. If anything, she cared too much.

He thrust a hand through his hair. "I don't understand. You've been helping me get them back. The other day at the newspaper, you—"

"Why do you have to do this, Rafe?" Her hands abandoned her stomach to reach out to him. "Aren't I enough for you?"

"What the hell are you talking about? Of course you're enough for me. I love you, damn it."

"Do you? Or do you love the me I used to be?"

Rafe blinked hard in surprise. All the things that had been niggling at the edges of his comfort zone suddenly made sense— all the comments she'd been making over the past week about how great things were now, all the times he'd wanted to talk about the past and she changed the subject.

As if she needed to drive home her point, she continued. "I love you just the way you are now. I don't need the Rafe from the past. I don't need to remember anything about him, because I want the man you are today. Can't you do the same for me?"

"It's easy to say you don't need to remember when you can remember anything you want." His words were soft, but had underpinnings of cold, hard steel.

"You remember me from the past."

"But I don't remember everything. I can't go forward until I reach back and retrieve all my past. You're the only one who can help me do that. Go with me."

Tears shone in her eyes. "Rafe, please—"

He grasped her shoulders. "I don't understand what you're afraid of, Emma. How can I separate the two of you? Part of you *is* the past. I loved you six and a half years ago for who you were then, and I love you today for who you are now."

"Then don't ask me to go to Houston."

Rafe couldn't believe what he was hearing. He felt betrayed on the most basic level—as if he didn't know this woman at all. "Why don't you want me to have my memories?"

She pressed her lips together.

"You've helped me all along," he pointed out.

"Not because I wanted to."

His head jerked as if she'd slapped him, but that's exactly how he felt. "I thought you loved me."

"I do."

"No, you don't. If you loved me, you'd want me whole. If for no other reason than it's what I want."

Her voice held a thin edge of desperation. "Why is the past so important? The past doesn't matter. It can't be changed. Only today matters, and tomorrow. We didn't have any tomorrows until you came back to Memphis. Now we do. Are you going to throw that away just so you can remember the name of a dog you had when you were ten years old?"

Rafe read straight through her words to the fear seething beneath. "You're afraid I don't love you, that I'm going to leave you."

Her eyes widened. "If you loved me, I'd be enough for you. Me. Now. The way I am."

He knew exactly what her fear meant. It was what he'd been fighting against ever since he found her, what he thought he'd conquered. "You still don't trust me."

"I...I love you, Rafe."

She couldn't even lie about it.

"What's love without trust? About as substantial as the wind."

"Please—"

"Go with me to Houston."

She pressed her lips together and searched his face. "If I go, I might lose you."

His eyes narrowed. "What the hell do you mean by that?"

"I mean that if you recall your past, you'll return to reporting. Then one day you'll go some place like Nicaragua again. And you might—"

He threw up his hands. "I'm not going back to reporting. I've told you and Jay and Ham over and over again. I'm not going to turn my back on *Southern Yesteryears,* and I'm not going to turn my back on you."

Sadness filled her eyes. "I saw you at the newspaper, Rafe. You remembered all the good times, how exciting it was, and you wanted it again."

Her words felt like a knife in his heart. She didn't believe him. He could talk until his throat gave out, assuring her he wasn't going to leave her, but she still wouldn't believe him. As he'd told her on the porch that night—he couldn't prove he wouldn't hurt her in the future. He could only show her. But that's what he'd been trying to do for over a month.

It all came down to trust. If she didn't trust him now, she probably never would.

"If you don't go to Houston with me, you'll definitely lose me." His statement was deliberately harsh, deliberately final. He needed to shock her into realizing how much this meant to their future happiness. If she couldn't trust him, there'd be no future at all, so they might as well end it now.

Her eyes widened. "What?"

"We're about to recommit our lives to each other, but I need a commitment from you right now. I need to know you trust me so much you'd fly to the moon in a spaceship I built with my own hands. I need to know you love me enough to stand by me no matter what the future brings. Even if I decided to go back to reporting, which I won't, I need to know you'll be there beside me, wanting what I want. Haven't I given you what you want? Have I made one single decision without you? Have I at any time tried to take control of your life or Gabe's?"

She looked away.

He took a deep breath. "Go to Houston with me tomorrow, Emma. Please."

Emma's world whirled around her, but inside she was utterly still, utterly dead. How could this be happening? How could she have found Rafe after all these years, only to lose him again so soon?

She needed more time—time to make him love her enough. But time was the one thing she didn't have.

She was damned if she went and damned if she stayed.

If she went, she knew with dreadful certainty he'd eventually return to reporting—no matter what he said. She'd been there. She'd seen the longing on his face. He'd put himself into the kind of situation like the one in Nicaragua—the kind of situation that would probably kill him.

If she didn't go, he'd leave her now.

But at least he'd be alive. At least she'd know he shared the same planet she did. At least there would be hope.

"Stay with me," she pleaded one last time. "Your parents will be here in two weeks. Won't that be soon enough?"

Rafe closed his eyes in a grimace of pain. After a long, agonizing moment, his dark eyes finally refocused on her face. In their dark depths, she couldn't find the smallest shred of hope for any future.

"I'll send someone to move my things." He stepped woodenly off the porch.

"Rafe, wait! Where are you going?"

"Home," he said. "To Houston."

The words cut deep. "Why? You can't get your memories back without me."

"Apparently the magic I thought I had with you was just an illusion. If I can create one, I can create another." He dug his keys out of his pocket. "Tell Gabe I'll call him tomorrow."

Chapter Twelve

Emma watched the clock on the computer screen tick off another minute. That made ninety-seven since, like a wounded animal, she'd retreated to her lair. To the place where she was comfortable, where she was in control.

She thought she'd be able to lose herself in work, but she hadn't gotten further than turning on the computer.

Rafe was gone.

The phrase echoed over and over in her empty mind, but her brain had yet to comprehend the message.

Maybe it just couldn't accept the fact that she would never hear him call her *querida,* never kiss his smiling lips, never run her hands down the rough skin of his back, never feel him inside her. Never again.

She sobbed, her throat so choked it barely admitted enough air to stay alive.

No! If she gave in to the despair, she'd be crying for days, weeks, a lifetime. Better to bury the agony deep inside where it couldn't surface. That's how she'd survived before. It would work again. Eventually.

All she had to do was—

"Mom? Dad? You up here?"

Gabe's call made Emma start. He was here for his nighttime story? Already?

Her hands flew to her face. Both felt clammy, cold. Thank God she hadn't been crying. She would never be able to give her son a believable explanation for tears.

Gabe pushed open the apartment door. His gaze fell on her, then scanned the room. "Hi. Where's Dad?"

"He's...gone."

"Where?"

"He...Houston. He went home." No! her mind screamed. His home was here.

"To see Gramma and Grampa? He promised to take me next time he went. Did you know they have a pool right in their own backyard?"

Emma nodded.

"When's he gonna be back?"

Hope speared through Emma. Of course Rafe would return for Gabe. He'd never give up seeing his son.

If you don't go to Houston with me now, you'll definitely lose me.

His words slammed into her soul, dashing the brief flare of hope and raising her pain to unbearable levels. It surged through her like a tidal wave of acid, eating her alive.

"Mom? You okay?" Gabe laid an uncertain hand on her knee.

Emma opened her eyes. She hadn't heard him cross the room. Taking a deep breath, she hugged him. "I'll live."

Unfortunately.

"When's Dad going to be home?" Gabe repeated.

I'll send someone to move my things.

Images played through her mind. Signing divorce papers...again. Long days and nights when Gabe was spending custody time with his father. And worse, seeing Rafe when he came to pick up Gabe, having to talk to him and pretend she didn't still love him.

You'll never have to worry about us getting divorced, son. Because we never will.

"Mom?"

She focused on her son. "I don't know, honey. He said he'll call you tomorrow. Have you had your bath?"

Gabe shook his head. "I wanted to ask Dad something first."

"You'd better go take one. It's almost bedtime." She added hopefully, "You want me to help?"

Gabe rolled his eyes and turned toward the door. "Jeez, Mom."

She sighed regretfully, then called after him. "Be careful going down the stairs."

"Trust me, okay?"

He closed the door with more enthusiasm than finesse, but Emma barely noticed that or his footsteps clomping down the outside stairs.

Trust me, okay?

Is that what her son thought? That she didn't trust him?

Gabe's words were an echo of Rafe's. So much so, she had to ask herself a difficult question. Was it true? Was she so far gone that she couldn't even trust her own son?

No, that was ridiculous. Gabe was only five years old, for goodness' sake, and the issue here was a fall off a few steps, not a potential helicopter crash.

What's the difference?

Emma's eyes focused on the picture of Rafe as an angel, and she realized she'd been staring at it. It was as if he was speaking to her.

What *was* the difference? she asked herself. Gabe could be killed falling off a few steps, depending on how he landed. Anything could happen.

Her hands gripped the arms of the chair as those words echoed in her mind. *Anything could happen.*

Of course it could. Why hadn't she realized that before?

She was worried about Rafe dying alone in some jungle, but he could be killed in a car accident on the way to the airport.

With a monumental effort, she tamped down the panic making her long to race for her car and follow him, to make sure he arrived safely.

But she couldn't wrap Rafe up in a cocoon of safety any more than she could protect Gabe from every little bump in the sidewalk. Even if she could, neither of them would want her to. All they required was for her to be there to kiss away the pain when something happened.

She'd accepted that fact about Gabe as soon as he learned to walk. Why did she think that Rafe, a grown man, was any different?

No matter how much he teased her, she wasn't Rafe's guardian angel. She couldn't keep him from harm twenty-four hours a day. No matter where he chose to go, or what he chose to do, he was on his own. Just like Gabe was.

How could she offer Rafe any less than she offered Gabe?

When it came right down to it, everyone was on their own. All a person could hope for was someone to help them along the way, to love them, to hold them, to kiss away the pain if they ran into one of the bumps on the sidewalk of life.

Overwhelmed by her insight, Emma leaned back.

She'd told Rafe all they had was today and tomorrow, but that was only half true. All they had was today, right now, this minute. They weren't guaranteed anything more.

Hadn't she learned that when she'd thought Rafe had died? After she'd finally accepted he was gone, she'd longed to see him again for just a minute, just long enough to tell him she loved him.

Now here she was, throwing away what could turn out to be a lifetime with him. And why? Because she was afraid she'd lose him again, afraid she wouldn't have him for all her tomorrows.

Afraid. That was it in a nutshell.

He'd said she still didn't trust him, but that wasn't true. It was life she didn't trust.

Well, life could take all its tomorrows and stuff them down its throat. She wanted Rafe in her arms, and she wanted him now.

Yes, he might return to the newspaper, and he might someday be killed doing his job. But that was true whether he was a reporter for the *Commercial Appeal* or editor of *Southern Yesteryears*. She wasn't going to throw away today just because she was afraid life would take him away tomorrow.

If you loved me, you'd want me whole.

Of course she loved him, and though she truly didn't care if he never got another memory, he cared.

How selfish she'd been, worrying that he didn't love her for the woman she was now. Never once had she considered that if she loved him for the man he was, she'd want to give him what he needed so badly.

He'd given her what she needed. He believed in her, relied on her, trusted her. He'd let her be herself, let her choose what to do with her life, now she wouldn't let him choose what to do with his.

Selfish. Selfish. Selfish.

Well, her selfishness was officially over. From now on, the only thing she'd be selfish about would be wanting to spend all the time she could with Rafe. She'd never be ashamed of wanting him.

Emma scooted the chair closer to the desk and pulled the telephone book out of a drawer to look up the airline with a hub in Memphis. Surely an airline with so many flights would have another one to Houston tonight.

The airline representative told her she'd just missed the last one. The one Rafe was probably on. The next flight to Houston took off at nine the next morning.

She booked a seat.

With a final bump, the plane started its sharp ascent into the skies over Memphis. The last rays of the dying sun hit Rafe in the face as he watched the streetlights of Memphis blink on in the growing darkness. The downtown buildings jutted from the bluffs along the Mississippi, and the two bridges across the river looked like scenery from a toy train set.

The plane banked, cutting off his view.

He felt a sudden wrenching, as if he were literally ripped from the city below, as if the connection he'd finally found after so many years of wandering blindly around in his own empty mind had suddenly snapped.

But that had happened two hours ago, when Emma refused to give him back his life.

How could he have been so blind? He'd believed her completely. He'd been so sure she loved him, so certain she wanted what was best for him.

What he didn't understand was how she could've had such a profound effect on him—being the catalyst that brought back his memories—when she didn't want to do it. When all she cared about was making sure he loved her for the woman she was now.

What kind of thinking was that?

How could he not love her? Compared with the girl he remembered, Emma was much more mature, much more of a woman. She was beautiful, sweet, a wonderful mother, a loving daughter and an insatiable lover. What man in his right mind wouldn't prefer that over an insecure girl who'd basically wanted to be rescued from an abusive father?

Rafe smothered a groan as he realized the path his thoughts were taking. He still loved her. Knowing she didn't trust him, knowing she only wanted what was best for herself.

Yet...how could he blame her for being selfish? She hadn't had anyone to lean on, all of her life, except for the brief months they'd been together years ago. She'd learned to be defensive, to take care of herself—because nobody else had been taking care of her.

Sylvia was a gracious lady, but not a strong one. Not strong enough to stand up to a monster of a husband.

But Emma was strong. Strong enough to raise their son on her own. Strong enough to survive in a harsh world. Strong enough to help him recall his past, even though it scared her to death.

How could he not love her?

The question echoed in his heart, which told him that not loving her was impossible. He'd love her whether they were together or apart, whether he had his memories or not.

So it came down to one simple question: which was more important, Emma or his past?

He didn't even have to think. Emma was more important to him than anything else in the world, with the possible exception of Gabe. He'd lost her once. Now he'd do anything to keep her in his life, including giving up part of his.

What were memories compared to her? They couldn't keep him warm at night. They couldn't kiss him or hold him or love him. The past wasn't what was going to make him whole. Emma was what made him complete. She was the other half of his soul. The piece of him that had been missing for over six years.

She was right. The past didn't matter. What mattered was that they were together for the rest of their lives.

And he was speeding away from her at five hundred miles an hour.

Rafe threw his head back against the narrow seat with a grimace as a sudden realization hit him.

This was their first fight since they'd recommitted themselves to each another and what had he done? Cut bait and run.

He'd done exactly what Emma had been afraid of all along. She believed men didn't have what it took to stick around, that the only way they could operate was "their way or the highway." The men in her life had solved their problems by controlling her, by forcing her to their way of thinking.

Like he'd tried to do.

Damn, damn, damn, damn, damn.

She had every right not to trust him.

He had to get back to her. Tonight. He had to prove that he was going to stick around for the rest of her life, no matter what happened.

He couldn't get discouraged by the fact that she didn't trust him. Her mistrust had built up over years of emotional abuse. He couldn't expect to overcome that in a month. It might take years, but he didn't care. He was patient, and he was stubborn. One day, she'd trust him. He was going to make it his mission in life.

He landed in Houston at ten. Since he had no luggage, he went straight to the ticket counter. There wasn't another flight to Memphis on any airline until the red-eye at six-thirty the next morning.

He booked a seat, then resisted the urge to call Emma. What needed to be said needed to be said in person.

He decided against calling his parents, too. They didn't know he was flying in tonight. No sense in disturbing them. If they came to get him, they'd have to bring him right back in just a few hours.

So he bought a bestseller at the only newsstand open late, found a reasonably comfortable seat and sat down to wait out the night.

Rafe reined in his impatience as passengers hauled down their overhead luggage and meandered into the Memphis airport. Because he'd bought his ticket late last night, he'd had a seat all the way in the rear.

He was anxious to get home to Emma. Through the long night, he'd been coming up with all kinds of things Emma's mistrusting mind might be convincing her of—like he'd never loved her, like he'd just been using her to regain his memories.

Why couldn't he have realized what he was doing before he'd gotten on that stupid plane?

Rafe shoved the self-reprimand aside. He'd had that argument with himself all night, too, and there was no answer.

Finally he saw the light at the end of the jetway. He squeezed past several slow-moving passengers and past the gate.

Three strides out, he stopped so suddenly a man behind bumped into him. Rafe barely noticed. The only thing he saw was Emma sitting in the second row of seats.

He shook his head to clear it, but she was still there, rising slowly to her feet, her eyes wide.

Rafe? He saw her mouth his name, but the noisy crowd and airline announcements drowned out the sound.

Two more strides brought him close enough to enfold her in his arms. Her arms wrapped around him, so tight he thought she'd never let go.

Thank God.

"I'm sorry. I'm sorry. I'm sorry. I'm sorry."

When they realized they were uttering the litany in unison, they pulled apart enough to smile nervously at each other.

Still amazed to find her here, Rafe pushed a strand of hair from her cheek. "How did you know I was coming in?"

"I didn't." She twisted and pulled a ticket from her purse. "I'm about to get on a plane to Houston."

Rafe glanced at the ticket, then searched her beautiful, loving face. Joy exploded in his chest like fireworks. She was going to Houston. She did trust him. She did love him.

He couldn't resist tasting her lips. "I love you."

"I love you, too."

He smiled. "I know."

"What—" Emma was jostled from behind.

Rafe glanced up to glare at a man bent over to get something out of his carry-on bag. Realizing they stood in the middle of a crowded airport gate, Rafe took Emma's hand and drew her down the terminal to a deserted area. He pulled her into a corner and into his arms.

"That's better. Now we can talk."

"What are you doing here?" she demanded. "You went to Houston, didn't you?"

He nodded. "Then I took the first plane back."

"You did?" It was like a switch had suddenly been turned on, making her face shine with love.

He nodded. "As soon as I was in the air, I realized I was making a huge mistake. You're right, *querida*. The past doesn't matter. What matters is that you're in my arms right now, and that you stay here."

"Oh, Rafe." Emma was suddenly blinded by tears. It humbled her to realize how much he was willing to give up because he loved her. "Your memories—"

"Damn my memories." He tightened his hold. "They aren't what makes me whole. You do."

The tears spilled over the brink of her lids. "That's the most beautiful thing anyone's ever said to me."

He kissed her temple. "Let's go home, *mi corazón*."

He started to pull her down the terminal, but Emma dug in her heels. "No."

He stopped and arched a brow at her.

"We're going to Houston," she told him firmly. "On the next plane."

He smiled sadly. "You don't have to do this, *querida*. I told you—"

"I know what you told me, but you're wrong. The past does matter, at least to you. So we're going to Houston so you can have all of your memories."

"But—"

"Let me do this for you. Please." She lovingly ran a finger down the scar on his face. "You've done so much for me."

"I thought you were worried I'd go back to reporting."

"I still am. But if that's what you want to do, I'll bravely kiss you goodbye and send you on your way." She smiled wryly. "I'll worry the whole time you're gone and make you call me every hour on the hour, but—"

He pulled her close. "I'm not going back to reporting. Never. Understand?"

She put her fingers across his lips. "Hush. We don't know what the future will bring. All we have is today. Let's just be glad we're together now."

"I'm not going back to reporting," he insisted. "I need you to trust me on this, Emma."

She was amazed to realize she did. "I do trust you. Isn't that remarkable? I haven't felt like this in years. I feel so...light. So free." She threw her arms around his neck and kissed him thoroughly on the mouth. "Thank you, *querido*. You've given me back the ability to trust, something I thought I'd lost forever."

"So now you're like you were when we were married, aren't you? Is it all right for me to love you for who you were then, because that's who you are now?"

She gave him a crooked smile. "You can love me any way you want to. Just love me."

Taking her face between his hands, he gave her a solemn kiss. "The way I love you is forever."

"But—"

"I know you said we don't have any guarantee of tomorrow. But I know I love you now, and I know I'll love you a minute from now. And that minute I know I'll love you the next minute, and so on, and so on, until our souls merge after eons in Heaven."

She could barely speak past the emotion constricting her throat. "Talk about pressure. I guess I have to be good the rest of my life, don't I? So I can be in Heaven with my angel. Maybe your wings will be healed by then."

He shook his head. "My wings are already healed. Your love and Gabe's love have made me whole. My family is all I need. Now let's go home."

"What about my ticket to Houston?"

"Let's trade it in on a ticket to the Bahamas. Or would you rather go to the mountains on our honeymoon?"

She laced her fingers with his as they turned toward the terminal. "Now that your wings are healed, why don't you just fly us?"

"Maybe I will, *querida*." He leaned down to kiss her. "At the moment, I feel like I could."

* * * * *

Look for Martha Shields's next
heartwarming Silhouette Romance,
THE PRINCESS AND THE COWBOY.
Our special **VIRGIN BRIDES** *title,*
in November 1999.

If you enjoyed what you just read,
then we've got an offer you can't resist!

Take 2 bestselling love stories FREE!

Plus get a FREE surprise gift!

Clip this page and mail it to Silhouette Reader Service™

IN U.S.A.	IN CANADA
3010 Walden Ave.	P.O. Box 609
P.O. Box 1867	Fort Erie, Ontario
Buffalo, N.Y. 14240-1867	L2A 5X3

YES! Please send me 2 free Silhouette Romance® novels and my free surprise gift. Then send me 6 brand-new novels every month, which I will receive months before they're available in stores. In the U.S.A., bill me at the bargain price of $2.90 plus 25¢ delivery per book and applicable sales tax, if any*. In Canada, bill me at the bargain price of $3.25 plus 25¢ delivery per book and applicable taxes**. That's the complete price and a savings of over 10% off the cover prices—what a great deal! I understand that accepting the 2 free books and gift places me under no obligation ever to buy any books. I can always return a shipment and cancel at any time. Even if I never buy another book from Silhouette, the 2 free books and gift are mine to keep forever. So why not take us up on our invitation. You'll be glad you did!

215 SEN CNE7
315 SEN CNE9

Name _____ (PLEASE PRINT)

Address _____ Apt.# _____

City _____ State/Prov. _____ Zip/Postal Code _____

* Terms and prices subject to change without notice. Sales tax applicable in N.Y.
** Canadian residents will be charged applicable provincial taxes and GST.
   All orders subject to approval. Offer limited to one per household.
   ® are registered trademarks of Harlequin Enterprises Limited.

SROM99   ©1998 Harlequin Enterprises Limited

Silhouette ROMANCE™

twins
on the doorstep

STELLA BAGWELL

continues her wonderful stories of the Murdocks
in Romance & *Special Edition!*

MILLIONAIRE ON HER DOORSTEP—May 1999
(SR#1368)

Then be sure to follow this miniseries when it
leaps into Silhouette Special Edition® with
Sheriff Ethan Hamilton, the son of Rose and
Harlan. Discover what happens when a small
New Mexico town finds out that...

PENNY PARKER'S PREGNANT!—July 1999
(SE#1258)

Judge Penny Parker longed to be a mother, but
the lonely judge needed more than the sheriff's
offer of a "trial" marriage....

Look for a new Murdocks short story in
Silhouette's Mother's Day collection, coming out in
May 2000

Available at your favorite retail outlet.

Silhouette®

Coming in June 1999 from

Silhouette Books ...

Those matchmaking folks at Gulliver's Travels are at
it again—and look who they're working their magic
on this time, in

HOLIDAY Honeymoons

Two Tickets to Paradise

For the first time anywhere, enjoy these two new
complete stories in one sizzling volume!

HIS FIRST FATHER'S DAY   Merline Lovelace
A little girl's search for her father leads her to
Tony Peretti's front door...and leads *Tony* into the
arms of his long-lost love—the child's mother!

MARRIED ON THE FOURTH   Carole Buck
Can summer love turn into the real thing? When
it comes to Maddy Malone and Evan Blake's
Independence Day romance, the answer is a
definite "yes!"

Don't miss this brand-new release—
HOLIDAY HONEYMOONS: Two Tickets to Paradise—
coming June 1999, only from Silhouette Books.

Available at your favorite retail outlet.

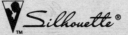

Silhouette®

This June 1999, the legend
continues in Jacobsville

Diana Palmer

LONG, TALL TEXANS
EMMETT, REGAN & BURKE

This June 1999, Silhouette brings readers
an extra-special trade-size collection
for Diana Palmer's legion of fans.
These three favorite Long, Tall Texans
stories have been brought back in
one collectible trade-size edition.

Emmett, Regan & Burke are about to be led
down the bridal path by three irresistible women.
Get ready for the fireworks!

Don't miss this collection of favorite
Long, Tall Texans stories…
available in June 1999
at your favorite retail outlet.

Then in August 1999 watch for
LOVE WITH A LONG, TALL TEXAN
a trio of brand-new short stories featuring
three irresistible Long, Tall Texans.

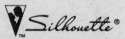